Katie

IN WAITING

- a novel -

D1715059

Erynn

Mangum

OTHER NOVELS
BY ERYNN MANGUM

THE LAUREN HOLBROOK SERIES

Miss Match

Rematch

Match Point

Match Made

Bake Me A Match

THE MAYA DAVIS SERIES

Cool Beans

Latte Daze

Double Shot

THE PAIGE ALDER SERIES

Paige Torn

Paige Rewritten

Paige Turned

Erynn Mangum

To my sweet family, especially my Jon – I could not have done this without your help and constant support.
Love you more than I can say.

A HUGE thank you to Mom, Cayce and Jen – such simple words don't begin to cover it! For everything you all have done to make this book what it is, I appreciate it!!
Love you all!

CHAPTER *One*

My alarm goes off at 6:47am. I roll over, smash the snooze button and lay there, blinking away the sleep from my eyes in my still-dark apartment.

It wasn't supposed to be like this.

I mean, yes, my alarm was supposed to go off at 6:47. Actually, I must have already hit snooze in my sleep once, because it's supposed to first go off at 6:40. Which is exactly the reason that I set three alarms. Usually by the second or third time, I actually wake up.

The thing that isn't going as planned? My *life*.

I had it all planned out, see. I was the one that carried around a planner even in middle school and my life was scheduled out in the back like an "I Before E" rule chart.

Junior Year – Start taking extra credit English classes for college credit

Senior Year – Graduate high school with college acceptance letter in hand

College – Graduate with honors before I'm 22

22 years – Get a well-paying job, save 40% of earnings for in a high yield account

23 years – Meet future husband, date for 2 years

25 years – Get married

27 years – Get pregnant, put job on hold until baby goes to pre-K

I had even written it all in one of those fine-point Sharpies. Those are supposed to count for something.

And yet, here I am. Thirty-one tomorrow. I did graduate college with honors. Twice, actually. I got my degree in English and then went back for my Masters. And I did get a great job. I actually work primarily from home doing editing work for Townsend and Mitchell, one of the largest publishers in the United States.

And that's pretty much where my schedule went off track.

I think I've been on maybe four dates in my entire life and none of them were anything to write home about. Seriously. I never even texted my mom about them. Two were men I'd met from work or work-related events. One was a guy from one of the churches I was visiting. And the other was a blind date from a well-meaning older woman at the New York office who I decided obviously didn't know me at all once I met the guy. I have no intention of relocating and neither did he. And we live a thousand miles apart.

It was going nowhere.

I roll out of bed and go straight for the shower. I have a lot of colleagues who have told me that the best part of working from home is getting to work in your pajamas, but I'm not about that. If I'm going to be working, I'm going to feel like I'm working. So I get up on time, I get dressed in actual, fitted clothing, I eat breakfast, get a cup of coffee and go into my home office.

It helps me separate the work and home a little bit at least.

I recently moved to Carrington Springs, Missouri. It's a small town but it actually has a huge medical community since it's right by the Mississippi River and is a central location for four other smaller-ish towns. So, it's a fairly desirable location to live.

It's also where my mother grew up and my grandmother still lives here. So, when I was considering if I wanted to move and where to move to, it was always at the top of my list. Really, anywhere other than New York would have been great, but Carrington Springs has been perfect for me. The airport is within a twenty-minute drive and I know at least one in the flesh person. When you spend 90% of your communication dealing with people on the phone or over email, it's nice to actually see a face every so often. I usually have to commute back to New York at least once a month, but that just means that once a month I get to have real pizza and sometimes I catch a show. Considering the cost of living in Manhattan, I am still saving money.

Gram was happy, I was happy and Mom was too stressed out caring for my younger twin siblings she and Dad adopted a few years back to really notice that I didn't move back to my hometown. Not that I would have seen them much anyway. The twins just turned eleven and I'm fairly certain that they have an activity every single night of the week.

I've been here for two months and I really try to make it to Gram's house once week for dinner, usually on Friday nights unless I'm in New York. I need the company more than she does, I'm pretty sure. Gram's social calendar puts even some of my super outgoing classmates from school to shame.

I get out of the shower, dry off and blow dry my hair. I run a curling iron through it and then pull on my work clothes, including a sweater. I am still trying to get used to my thermostat in this house. We are knee-deep in October right now and my air conditioner was apparently on all night because it's about twenty degrees cooler in my house than outside.

October in Missouri is basically the equivalent to heaven. The humidity has pretty much disappeared, the temperatures are crisp without being frigid and the trees look like God dumped buckets of random colors all over them. They are gorgeous. Plus, when you go outside, you can breathe in and it's just the smell of the trees that comes to your nose. None of the smog and filth like in New York.

I go in the kitchen, make myself an English muffin with apricot jam, press the button for a cup of coffee on my coffeemaker and I'm done eating in ten minutes. I carry my cup of coffee to my office.

Time to start the day.

My house is small but it's just me and I don't need a big one. Honestly, I rented the house more for the location than anything else. It's right next to some great walking trails and it's only ten minutes from Gram. And it's the closest I could get to the airport without getting into the sketchier sides of Carrington Springs.

I turn on my computer and pull up the latest draft of the cozy mystery I'm working on. It's one of those weird mixes of romance and murder and it works as long as you aren't eating when you're reading it. The author can be too descriptive with both the crime scenes and the making out.

Maybe my problem is I haven't found any dead bodies in my kitchen recently.

Probably if that happened, I'd find an adorably attractive and super tough cop who was by some miracle still single though he looked like a cross between Thor and Bradley Cooper.

Too bad Carrington Springs isn't really known for their crime scenes. Or their attractive cops, come to think of it.

I start my work day by checking my email and there's one from head editor at Townsend and Mitchell.

Katie,

We need you in New York next Tuesday for a department meeting. See you then.

- Joe

Short and sweet. Sort of like Joe himself, actually. He's about five feet, four inches tall and a very kind man. For all the cutthroat editors I've met over the years, Joe is one of those rare people who genuinely loves his work and is actually really good at his job. He's pretty much the reason Townsend and Mitchell have consistently reached the bestseller charts because he has an eye for acquisitions and knowing when something is going to sell really well.

I'm thinking my current client's book may not be one of those, but I guess you never know. There are always the surprises in publishing.

I schedule my flight and go back to my inbox. Lots of junk emails mostly, a few questions from clients and yet another "hope to see you on Sunday" message from one of the churches I visited a few weeks ago.

It wasn't my style.

I don't know what my style is, exactly, but it was too small and I met too many people who asked me too many times if I was by myself or if I'd brought a boyfriend or husband.

Yeah, no, and thanks for rubbing it in.

I tuck my hair behind my ears and try to focus. *I am happy, I am healthy, Jesus loves me and that's enough.*

The thing is, sometimes it's just not.

It's just after noon and I'm taking a lunch break, going in the kitchen for some leftovers from Gram's the other night. I swear the woman does not know how to cook for just two people. Any time I eat over there, she sends me home with enough leftovers to feed me for an entire week.

I think she's not-so-secretly worried about whether or not I eat when she's not around. She's commented on my dress size many times and even though I point out every time that family genetics are in my favor, she doesn't seem to comprehend that. I even unearthed a picture of her in her twenties to prove to her

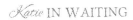

that I am not the only McCoy woman who looked like this, but she just blew me off.

"Those were different days," she said, waving her hand.

"Gram, it's the same genetics, though."

"Here, have another slice of peach pie, honey."

It was pointless.

I pop a bowl with the rest of the chicken casserole from her Pyrex dish in the microwave and set the pan in the sink to wash and return to her. It's Friday, so Gram's leftovers lasted me the entire week for lunch. I go to my front porch and get the mail out of the box, come back inside and set it on the table. The upside of working from home is I don't really have to make small talk with people I don't really want to talk to. The downside of working from home is I don't ever really get the chance to talk with people.

There's another postcard from yet another church I've tried. I've been slowly trying every church in Carrington Springs and I'm basically coming up completely dry. Either the church is too small, too big, too old or there are only young families and no one knows what to do with a woman in her thirties who, heaven forbid, is still single. One associate pastor kindly offered to start a singles class for me, but there is no way I'm going to a Sunday school class where I am the only person there.

Surely I am not the only 30-something, unattached person in all of Carrington Springs.

Surely. And if I am, I totally picked the wrong place to move. Maybe I should have reconsidered staying in New York.

I think about that for a little bit and shake my head.

It was fun for a time, but that time has passed.

And besides, if I think I have a rough time finding churches smack in the middle of the Bible belt, I need to remember what it was like in New York. New York is like Sin City compared to Carrington Springs. I couldn't find a church there to save myself. Possibly the biggest reason I moved. I just didn't think it would be this hard to find one now.

I take my casserole out of the microwave and sit at the table with a fork, spreading a magazine out on the table in front of me.

My house is quiet and it's just such a lonely sound.

I contemplated getting a dog at one point. Or a cat. Or something that cared if I was home or not. I'm just not a pet person. I think they smell bad and then they make your house smell, too. I had a friend back where my parents lived who had two cats and anytime I went into her house, all I could smell was litter boxes.

So nasty.

I did buy a plant three weeks ago. So now I do have something in the house who cares if I come home or not. I'm not even sure what kind of plant it is. I only know that it's super dramatic when it's been more than twelve hours since I watered it. Considering my total lack of a green thumb, I feel like I'm doing really well for having a plant live this long. I even killed a batch of succulents in my New York apartment and those are supposed to be dummy proof, according to Pinterest.

It wasn't the first time Pinterest let me down, though, so I wasn't overly upset about it. The whole white-on-white look that everyone has going on in their homes right now just isn't a practical look for someone who is known to carry coffee cups around the house, especially when coffee seems to have some sort of magnetic draw to white sofas.

I should have gone with the Scotch Guard like the lady at the furniture store suggested I do.

I look at the clock on the microwave, finish my last few bites and head back into the office. Time to get back to work. I'm supposed to be at Gram's by five o'clock, which she always complains is so late for dinner. Growing up, my family never ate dinner before seven since my dad was known to work late, so it just makes me laugh when it comes to Gram.

Five o'clock on the nose and I press the button for Gram's doorbell. She gave me a key three weeks ago, but it still just feels weird to let myself into her house. I only saw Gram once or twice a year for most of my childhood, so in a way, we are still trying to get to know each other.

"Honey, when are you going to start using that key?" Gram chides, opening the door.

"Hi Gram."

"You really should use the key. I gave you the key so you would use it and I wouldn't have to keep getting up to answer the door."

She says this like she sits in a rocking chair all day long but knowing her, I doubt she's sat down all day. Gram is a do-er. The woman doesn't stop from the second she wakes up in the morning until the minute she gets in bed at night. I bet if she doesn't have company, she even eats standing up.

I half hope I'm like this when I'm her age, but I also hope that by then, I can just relax a little bit.

"How was your day?" I ask her, following her and my nose into the kitchen. Gram lives in a house that is part of a retirement community. Her monthly payment includes one meal a day at the main building's dining room, but she still basically lives independently. There's also a pull-cord in a few places throughout the house, so if she needs help or falls, someone can be there in less than two minutes.

It's a great place for her and she has a ton of friends who also live here, so they stay busy organizing walks and fundraisers for different events and meals for the sick or injured. Add in her church activities, knitting club and gym membership and Gram could not be busier.

I mean, the woman has a personal trainer.

I've never had a personal trainer in my life. And I'm like the prime client for one. Thirties. Single. Cares about physical appearance. Money to burn.

Maybe I should sign up for one. I could meet my future husband at the gym.

All sweaty and flushed and gross with my hair sticking out all over the place.

How romantic.

"Wow, Gram!" I say, walking into the kitchen. She's made all my favorites. Chicken and dumplings, green bean casserole, frozen fruit salad and her homemade French bread. "Holy cow, this is a feast!"

Gram grins at me. "Happy early birthday, kiddo."

"Thanks, Gram." I was wondering if she knew or remembered. I wasn't going to say anything though, because can we be more awkward than, "Oh hey, Grandma, remember my birthday is this week?"

Yeah. I think not. Better to just quietly have dinner and leave.

But this is pretty much great.

Gram is patting my arm, like she usually does. "You are taking home all the leftovers and I've got three different pies and an angel food cake in the fridge."

I shake my head. "I am not taking all of this and three pies home."

"And the cake, honey. Don't forget about the cake."

"Gram, I'm going to have to spend all of my paycheck next week on new clothes if I eat all this stuff."

"Eh," Gram shrugs. "You work from home. Wear elastic. And besides, you are too thin. I saw this whole documentary on eating disorders two weeks ago."

This is something new that I'm getting used to. Gram and her documentaries. I don't know why Netflix hates us all, but my grandmother has watched almost every single one of the documentaries on there and I've had to make several lifestyle changes because of them.

The one about podiatric support about killed me. I love my flip flops.

I miss my flip flops. I couldn't hardly wear them in New York and I wore them every day here until Gram watched the documentary.

I'm hoping that by the time summer rolls around again, Gram will have forgotten about the dangers of improper arch support.

The odds aren't good. The woman is more than halfway into her eighties and remembers way more than I ever have in my entire life.

We fill up our plates with the goodness and sit at the island counter in her kitchen. The first time I came for dinner, Gram set the dining room table for me and used her best china and the real silver silverware and I felt super special, but also like company. You shouldn't feel like company at your grandmother's house. So, the next time I went, I took off my shoes at the door, handed her a stack of paper plates and told her we were eating in the kitchen where I knew she mostly ate anyway.

"So, did your mother call you yet?" Gram asks.

I finish chewing my bite of warm, soft on the inside, crusty on the outside bread and swallow, shaking my head. "I haven't talked to her in awhile." I can't actually remember the last time I talked to her, so that is probably a sign that it's time to call her.

Gram sighs. "She told me she would call you yesterday about it."

"She gets too busy with the twins. About what?"

"No, she *lets* herself get too busy with the twins. Just because there is two of them doesn't mean she needs to be constantly hand feeding them or working through every minor issue they come across. Goodness knows she didn't do that with you."

I smile. Mom and Dad adopted Micah and Mia when I was a junior in college. They were almost two at the time. It's been a circus at their house since.

"Anyway, do you remember your mother's friend Michelle?"

"I don't think I've ever met her, but I remember Mom talking about her."

"I'm sure she has. They were best friends growing up. If she wasn't at Michelle's house, then Michelle was over at our house. Anyway, Michelle's oldest daughter is getting married this weekend."

"Good for her."

Gram pats my hand holding my fork and makes me almost drop my dumpling. "God will bring the right man for you in His time, dear," she says.

"Mm," I say, because I'm not sure that will be the case, but it's better to just agree and move on when it comes to Gram.

"Well, I would love to go to the wedding but I had already committed to helping with the fall fundraiser at church that day, so I was going to see if you wouldn't mind going in my place."

I swallow again and take a drink of my ice water, shaking my head. "I don't know, Gram, I mean, I don't even know her. Or Michelle. Or the groom."

"Psh," Gram says, waving her hand. "At weddings these days, it doesn't matter if you know the couple or not. In my day, it did matter because they weren't the fifty thousand dollar galas that they are now where you can't even speak to the bride or groom because they are so tied to their wedding planner and the photographer. Did you know the average wedding these days costs over forty thousand dollars? Forty thousand! Why, your grandfather and I bought our first house for twenty and it was a small fortune then. I've even heard people are actually going into debt to pay for these ridiculous events. Just complete nonsense."

I grin. "Tell me how you really feel about weddings, Gram."

"Oh, I am all for weddings. Just not these one-uppers that everyone is doing these days." She pats my arm. "It's next Saturday and I would very much appreciate it if you would go. I have a gift for them already so you would only need to put on a pretty dress and sign the guest book. You don't even have to go to the reception, though I did RSVP before I realized that it was the same day as the fundraiser. These invitations these days are so hard to read. You need a decoder just to find out who is getting married."

I sigh. "I mean, I...maybe."

"You should do it. If nothing else, it's a free gourmet steak and a lobster tail that probably cost them eighteen dollars a plate. And they'll just be throwing it away because I already RSVP'd for it."

"Lobster?"

"Isn't that just ridiculous?"

"That's pretty fancy. I don't know, Gram. I mean, are you even allowed to invite people to take your invitation?"

"Please just do it, Katie? I'm sure they won't mind. And like I said, it's not like you'll even talk to them."

I sigh again, this time louder so I know she can hear me.

"Oh, stop grousing and eat your dumplings."

"Yes, ma'am."

CHAPTER *Two*

Sunday morning. My alarm on my cell phone goes off and I moan.

I do not want to go to church.

And besides, my birthday was yesterday. Now I am old.

Old and alone and nothing to show for it other than a rental house, a plant and an upcoming business trip on Tuesday.

I turn off the alarm, roll over and look at the ceiling.

"Lord, how bad would it be if I didn't go to church? What if You and I did church here in my house?"

Somehow, I feel like the church apostles would have probably preached a sermon to me on the importance of church fellowship if they'd heard my prayer.

But what if you can't find a church to fellowship in? I mean, sure, I've found a lot of churches but none that just felt *right*.

I don't even know how to explain it. I just know that when I find it, I'll know.

I push myself out of bed and stumble down the hall to my office where I'd left my list of churches in town. I'd made a list when I first moved here of churches that fit the bill for me theologically – at least according to their websites – that I wanted to try.

Six down, three to go.

My odds weren't good.

I tried Gram's church the first week I was here and while it was really fun to meet all her friends, it definitely did not have very many younger people. If any. And while lunch at Molly's, one of the local cafés, was super great with all of them, I sort of felt like I was on display and not like I was visiting a church and trying to meet people.

I look at the name of the next church on the list. First Community Church of Carrington Springs. A big name for a likely little church. This isn't a huge town so the churches tend to be on the smaller-ish side.

Might as well go.

I take a shower, blow dry my hair and put on my now customary Trying A New Church outfit. Dark-rinsed jeans, a silky blouse top over a camisole and my brown leather ballet flats. I do a few curls in my hair with my curling iron and make sure I have my lipstick in my purse so I can put it on when I get into the church parking lot. And I took my time applying a little bit of blush to my cheeks today. One of the major disadvantages of an office job, especially one where you rarely leave your home, is that you tend to be a little on the pasty side.

I type in the address for the church on my map app and listen to the canned woman's voice telling me when to turn right and left on the way there. I make the last turn around a hill and feel my eyes widen.

And maybe there are bigger churches in Carrington Springs.

First Community Church is *huge*. I mean, the building looks like it ate the last three churches I visited.

Huge can be a good thing. It means you can have the feeling of fellowship, if not the practice of it.

Huge can also be a bad thing. Mostly because it means you can have the feeling of fellowship, if not the practice of it.

I park in the seventh packed row and slide my keys into my purse, pulling out my lipstick and grabbing my Bible. I always have a little bit of a nervous twinge in my stomach every time I try a new church and today is no exception. I finally figured out that eating my customary Sunday morning drive-thru Starbucks coffee cake and downing a caramel Frappucino wasn't helping, so I cut that out. Now, it's just normal to have the nervous twinge. On the plus side, I've lost two pounds, so I guess there are perks to always being on the church hop.

I mean, it's like Saint Peter himself is going to come back from the grave to lecture me.

The early church had it way better. No denomination drama and there weren't as many choices. And everyone was basically an eyewitness when it came to Jesus.

But then, they had to deal with some severe persecution.

Suddenly the denomination issue doesn't seem as big of a deal.

I walk up to the big front entrance and an equally big man is standing by the door with a smile that stretches six feet across.

"Good morning!" he bellows at me and shoves his ginormous hand towards me. "Welcome to First Community! Is today your first time with us?"

"Um, yes sir," I say and my voice sounds like a little mouse from a Beverly Cleary book compared to his booming baritone.

"Great!"

I have to hold myself back from jumping at his exclamation. Maybe I misread the website and First Community is actually a charismatic church.

Not that anything is wrong with that, I just like to be prepared.

"Well, here is a booklet about our church home and here's a pamphlet about how to know if you are saved and here's a free Bible and some mints and a free pen!" He piles my arms full of stuff and points me inside the building. "There's the sanctuary and I think our music pastor is warming up. So go on in and get yourself a seat!"

I walk inside and despite the crowds of people milling around, it's freezing cold in the building. Like ice cold. I'm immediately wishing for a jacket or a sweater or even one of Gram's shawls. Maybe the sanctuary isn't as cold.

Another smiling man hands me a bulletin to stack on top of the pile I'm already carrying and opens the sanctuary door and nope, it's possibly even colder in there than out in the crowded foyer.

Mental note. If I come back, I need to bring a parka.

I find a seat in the huge auditorium near the back and my butt barely hits the seat before the music starts in nice and loud. "Let's all stand and worship together," a man standing in front of a keyboard says into a microphone on the stage.

Next thing I know, like thirty people in purple silky robes come busting out from nowhere onto the stage and all of a sudden, it's like gospel music exploded in the air like a piñata overhead. People flood into the auditorium from the foyer and find their place in the row, though no one sits and almost everyone is swaying to the music, singing along with the choir and clapping or raising their hands.

What. In. The. World.

This is the absolute polar opposite of Gram's church. Like the only thing they have in common is the word "church" in their name. While Gram's church has music, it's very quiet and mostly hymns. There's only an organ too.

This place has a drum set and a bass player. Actually, strike that, they have two bass players.

It's so, so different.

But...

The music is catchy and I find myself tapping my toes as it continues. They sing four songs, congregation busting out in praise and me stumbling along as best as I can with the words on the screen. An older chocolate-skinned man with gray short hair comes out on the stage and preaches for about forty-five minutes in the book of 1 Peter. I'm taking notes furiously and realize I've never heard anyone explain the passages the way that he is. People are laughing at his stories, getting teary at his descriptions of God's love and I look around and see a sea of faces, all different colors, all different nationalities and all different ages.

It's refreshing, especially coming from a background where 97% of the people at my church growing up looked and acted exactly like my family.

We sing two more songs and church is dismissed.

I feel like I need to sit down or something even though I sat through the whole sermon.

"Hello there!" the lady who was sitting two seats down from me says, turning as we are all gathering our stuff. She looks at my pile and grins. "You must be new!"

"Yes, ma'am."

She waves a hand. "Ma'am. Please. Call me Charla. Charla Klein. And what's your name?"

"Katie. McCoy. Katie McCoy."

"Nice to meet you, Katie. Are you just new to First Community or new to Carrington Springs in general?"

"Both, I guess. I've lived here for about six weeks."

"Wonderful! What brings you to town?"

I'm cringing, waiting for the question that always, always comes about whether or not I'm married.

I tell her about my editorial job and how I decided since I could live anywhere, I might as well live close to my grandmother and the lady actually gets teary.

"Well, bless you, honey, that's just the most precious thing I ever heard."

She lays a hand on my shoulder and looks into my eyes and I swear she is reading the very depths of my soul before she squeezes me into a hug and says, "I love making new friends! So thankful you are here today, Katie. Now I'm saving this seat for you next week, okay then?"

I smile. "Okay."

I meet a good fifteen or twenty people on my way out the door because this church apparently shares Charla's enthusiasm for making new friends. By the time I'm sitting back in my car, my hand is shaking up and down of its own volition.

That was different.

And incredibly great.

I smile.

I will be back.

Early Tuesday morning, I hand a girl in a black polo shirt a ten dollar bill and she gives me two back.

Ridiculous how much coffee costs at the airport.

I sit down in front of my gate and wait, drinking my latte and people watching since I'm trying to save the magazines I bought for the flight. Business travel always sounded so much more glamorous before I was actually doing it. Now it's just time-consuming. And I miss my mattress. For as nice as the hotel that's right by Townsend and Mitchell is, it's still not home. And as much as I love a good New York pastry, it's not my bowl of Raisin Bran at home in my pajamas. So, business travel isn't what I thought it would be like.

But still way better than living in New York.

The meeting that Joe wants me to go to starts at two o'clock and will go through tomorrow until five o'clock at night. I'd considered trying to fly back home late tomorrow, but Joe insisted I stay an extra night and let the company take me out to a nice dinner.

I mean, if I have to get treated to what will likely be a five-star restaurant in New York City, then I guess I have to.

"All right folks, we are now boarding Flight 498 to St. Louis."

I gather my purse, my briefcase and my rolling suitcase. I don't check when I go to New York anymore unless it's for a week or longer. It's way too much of a pain.

I hand the agent my ticket and start the journey. From here to St. Louis is about a twenty minute puddle-jumper flight and I've got like a fifteen minute layover there. Basically long enough to run to the restroom and board my next flight. From St. Louis to New York, I am catching a non-stop that should get me to LaGuardia in about two and a half hours, then I have to take a taxi from LaGuardia to midtown Manhattan.

Assuming everything goes smoothly and there aren't any accidents on the bridge, I should make it with time to spare for the meeting. The office is located fairly close to Central Park.

By noon, I'm loading my suitcase into the back of a taxicab and telling the driver the address of Townsend and Mitchell. When I first moved to New York, I used to get incredibly nervous traveling in taxis alone, but now it's so normal that I don't even really think twice about it. I look out the window as we cross the bridge and it hits me all over again just how huge New York really is in such a small, small space.

"And here we are, miss," the driver says.

"Thanks." I check the meter, hand him the cash and climb out, feeling like I smell like a taxi and a plane now, which isn't the best combination. But the air outside the cab is crispy and full of smells ranging from the fresh scents of the Park to the mouth-watering aromas coming from the bakeries close by to the smoggy, smoky heaviness of the city.

There really is nothing like New York City in the fall.

The trees are turning colors in Central Park and people are already wearing their long jackets because in Midtown, everything is a matter of fashion if not practicality.

Unless you're a tourist.

Sometimes I watch them and wonder how much I stuck out like a sore thumb when I first started working here.

"Katie!" Joe is waving at me as I get off the elevator on the nineteenth floor. "How was the flight? I still can't believe you up and left us, by the way." He takes my suitcase and briefcase from me and carries them into his office, not stopping long enough for me to answer his question about the flight. "So Jack Jamison wants to revise his thriller *again* and this is going to set back our release date another three months. Dan is so mad he could scream. And he does, actually, only it's at me and not at Jack."

"I'm sorry, Joe."

"How's Sue's cozy mystery coming?"

"It's coming." I am about halfway through it. It's good except for the descriptions. "I'm going to need to scale her back on the adjectives."

Joe grins. "I told Sue that last time too."

I'd forgotten Joe had worked with this author on her previous series we'd published.

We leave my stuff in his office, I go wash up and attempt to get the smell of the plane and taxi off of me in the restroom with my perfume and then it's time to start the meeting. Editorial meetings are always long but Townsend and Mitchell tend to cater high quality snacks to keep us all awake, so that's nice, especially since I didn't have lunch. I load up a plate with freshly-cut veggies and some sort of incredible dip and then around four o'clock, a gigantic box of cupcakes from Magnolia Bakery shows up.

Bless these people.

I pick the crumbs out of the paper liner and look around the conference table, wondering if it would be super rude of me to get another cupcake, especially since Janet, the editor I'm sitting next to, is recently gluten-free and just kept sighing sadly at my first one.

The room we are in has one wall of just windows looking out over Central Park. We have most of the editorial staff in here today and it's always nice to see everyone in person instead of trying to communicate over email and text.

A lot of the editors here work from home. When I moved, Townsend and Mitchell had just revised their company guidelines on working from home and it made it super easy for me to make the change. A few, like Joe, still work in house. I think Janet does. I know Maggie, one of the older editors who has tried to set me up at least six times with the oddest people ever, still works in house.

Actually, strike that. The men Maggie set me up with are not the oddest ever. I forget sometimes some of the characters I've met in this city.

The meeting concludes at six and people start to slowly scatter. Most of the people are just in town for the meeting so we have no place to rush off to, other than a boring hotel room. Of the people who live here, I think only two or three are actually married with families. New York does not promote a great family life. I've seen the poor moms struggling with car seats and strollers plus their children in the taxis. It's awful and it totally validates every person I've ever known leaving this city the moment they find out they are pregnant.

A few of us milling around end up deciding to go get pizza at John's Pizzeria in Times Square and I don't get back to my hotel room until close to ten, stuffed with cheese, dough and tiramisu. Tomorrow's meeting starts early and I'll have to update everyone on the latest with the cozy mystery, so I head right to bed.

I lay down on the mattress and look up at the ceiling. Sometimes, I find myself wondering if I made the right move, leaving the bright lights and busyness of New York for the quiet, boring Carrington Springs. In New York, no one cared if you were single because likely, they were as well. Unlike Carrington Springs, where if you didn't have a husband and a family and you were over a certain age, people just didn't know what to do with you.

"Lord, did I do the right thing?"

Either the heavens are quiet or I just can't hear God through the noise of the city, which never turns off.

I roll over and fall asleep to the sound of horns honking, engines revving and a random yell or whistle here and there.

CHAPTER *Three*

Back in Carrington Springs and I'm tired.

Tired and ready to sleep in my own bed. I've only been away from the noise of New York for six weeks and I'm already used to the quiet. My head is pounding as I get off the plane, find my car in the parking garage and head home. I flick off the radio and just breathe in the stillness as I drive.

This.

This is confirmation enough for me. So maybe there isn't as much excitement and I'll never meet a single man my age. At least there isn't constant, constant noise.

I think about the people I left behind and shake my head. Not one good friend. Sometimes I wonder if I'd had close friends out there if I would have stayed.

Not that I have friends here either.

Hopefully with time.

Hopefully.

I get home, throw my suitcase, briefcase and purse on the couch and go in the kitchen to see what I have in the fridge for dinner. It's Thursday so I'm usually running low on leftovers from Gram's and groceries but since I've been gone, I haven't eaten as much, so chicken and dumplings it is.

Yay.

I put the bowl in the microwave and then open up my computer to check my personal email. Nothing much is here. A bunch of spam, more emails from churches I've visited and a quick one-liner from Gram:

Don't forget about the wedding this Saturday. I'll give you the gift at dinner on Friday. Love you. Gram.

The wedding. I had almost forgotten.

Kind of wish I had forgotten. I mean, how awkward is it to go to a wedding when you don't even know the people? Isn't that the definition of a wedding crasher? Wasn't there a movie made about that?

The microwave beeps and I eat my dumplings, carrying the bowl around my house as I open blinds and get the house back to normal. It's only four o'clock but after eating lunch at ten o'clock this time, I'm starving.

I open my front blinds and there's a mid-sized U-haul truck parked across the street. Apparently, the owners finally rented out that house. It's been sitting vacant for almost a year, according to my next door neighbor. I squint out the window at the people unloading the truck, feeling like a nosy old woman.

A good-looking, younger-ish man walks down the gangplank, two huge boxes stacked on top of each other in his arms and a pretty brunette about the same age is right behind him with two large garbage bags.

Looks like a young married couple is moving in. I wonder if they have kids? Or a dog? I look at the man again. Or maybe even an older, single brother?

I remember the church I went to in New York doing a series on singleness. Half of the congregation was single there and it was pretty much normal. No one was really looking to get married and everyone was looking to advance their career. I remember the pastor talking about how "noble a calling" singleness was and how Jesus and Paul were both single as well so we were in the best of company.

I remember looking around and noticing that nobody cared. No one thought singleness was a bad thing in New York. If anything, people viewed relationships and marriage as the downfalls.

It was different for me. Even when I was tiny, I always would pretend to be married. I had three baby dolls and they were my children and they all had names and birthdays and likes and dislikes. I wanted nothing more than to grow up and be a wife and mom.

I shake my head and leave the window, setting my empty bowl in the sink. My biological clock alarm went off years ago.

Guess I need to be neighborly.

I pull out the flour, white and brown sugars, butter, salt and baking soda and start mixing up a batch of chocolate chip cookies. If nothing else, at least I can cram these in my mouth while crying at the ending of *While You Were Sleeping* tonight for the forty-third time.

Maybe I need to follow Sandra Bullock's lead and start searching the hospitals around here for coma patients. I mean, I do live in a booming medical metropolis.

Maybe I should have been a nurse. Isn't that supposed to be like the most romantic profession? Smoothing back handsome patients' hair while they run ridiculously high fevers and fall desperately in love with me?

No more *Grey's Anatomy* for me. I pull out my beaters and start creaming the butter together with the sugars. Twenty minutes later, I pull out the first batch of cookies, let them cool slightly on the pan and then set them on a paper towel to cool the rest of the way while I work on the next batch. I get five dozen cookies out of the recipe.

I pull out a paper plate and Saran Wrap and put two dozen still-warm cookies on the plate, wrapping it lightly with the plastic wrap since the chocolate chips are still all melty. I find my shoes, try to wipe off the extra mascara under my eyes thanks to a long morning of flying and spray on some scented spray so I don't smell quite so much like stale plane air.

It's gorgeous weather today. Barely a cool breeze, probably close to seventy degrees and there are picture perfect white fluffy clouds dotting the blue sky. The trees are gold and red and orange and it smells crisp and clean.

As much as I love New York in the fall, it's just so much better here.

The man is halfway down the gangplank when I cross the street. "Hi there," I say, mustering up a friendly, happy smile. "Are you guys moving in?"

"I'm not," the man says. "But yes, she is." He nods in this weird backward way to the woman in the truck behind him and goes the rest of the way down the gangplank to the garage where he sets down his boxes.

She pokes her head out. "I thought I heard another voice out here!" she says, grinning, stepping onto the tailgate and jumping down to the ground beside me.

Up close, she looks a little older, probably close to my age. She shoves her hand out to me, using the other hand to try and stick a wayward lock of auburn brown hair back into the messy bun she has on the top of her head.

"Eliza Wakeman," she says, smiling.

"Katie McCoy," I say, shaking her hand. "I live across the street. Welcome to the neighborhood."

"Thanks!" She pushes her hands in her jeans pockets and looks around. "It's a beautiful city. I'm really excited to be here!"

"You just moved to Carrington Springs?"

"Yep! Just took a job at Northeast Hospital."

"Really?"

She nods. "I'm a nurse."

Of course she is. Well, maybe she can help me find the coma patient.

She's still talking. "I've spent the past few years in St. Louis working a night shift but you know, I've always wanted a day shift and one came up here and it just sounded like a great big adventure, so I just took it."

She's grinning the whole time she's talking and I happen to catch a glimpse of the man shaking his head as he walks back up into the truck.

"So, anyway, that's why I'm here! What do you do?"

"I'm an editor. I work from home, so if you ever need anything, the odds are good that I'll be around unless I'm in New York for a meeting."

"New York!" she gasps. "Oh I love New York! It's beautiful!"

"And dirty. And totally unsafe," says the man, carrying another two gigantic boxes down the gangplank. Now that I'm closer to him too, he also looks older. And based on the way he's looking at Eliza, I'm betting he's a sibling.

Probably an older brother.

Eliza rolls her eyes. "Don't listen to him, he's never been there."

"Lize, I was with you on the same trip, remember?"

"Yeah, but there's a difference between enjoying it and just scowling the whole time."

"So because I didn't enjoy it, that means I didn't actually go?"

"Pretty much."

He sets the boxes down in the garage. "So does that mean you've never been camping?"

She makes a face. "Blegh. And you complain New York is dirty. At least there is running water in New York."

He sighs and shakes his head, then wipes his hand on his jeans and sticks it out to me. "Mike Wakeman. Eliza's older brother."

"Katie," I nod. I hand Eliza the plate of cookies. "These are for you guys."

"Oh wow! Oh, this is so sweet of you! Thank you so much!" She grins at me. "I'm going to run these inside before they melt in the sun. Be right back."

She disappears through the open front door.

Mike watches her go and then looks at me. "Look, you seem fairly normal. Keep an eye on her, will you? It makes me nervous her living here all by herself."

"In the house or in Carrington Springs?"

He shrugs. "Both, I guess. She's never lived in a whole house by herself. And it's just too far away for me to get here if something happens."

I nod. "I'll keep an eye out. But honestly, you don't have much to worry about in Carrington Springs."

"I mean, if her toilet floods, she's not going to have the first clue of what to do."

"I have a plunger."

"Or what if the ceiling leaks? Or her brakes stop working in her car? Or she forgets to pay the mortgage on time?"

"Is she prone to forgetting her payments?"

"I hope not."

I nod to Mike. "She'll be fine, Mike. Don't worry about her."

He huffs his breath out. "Right."

I smile. There's something really sweet about an over-protective brother. "Do you live in St. Louis?"

"Yeah." He runs a hand through his tousled hair that is the same color as his sister's. "Too far."

"It's just a couple of hours."

"Long enough to flood her house."

I try to hide the smile. "I've been here for six weeks and haven't had any flooding issues yet. And I've been here through a rain storm. If her house floods, she can come stay with me until the waters recede."

"And the brakes?"

"I imagine they have mechanics here in Carrington Springs."

Eliza comes back out and she is eating a cookie. She hands one to Mike and he takes a bite, frowning.

"Oh my gosh, Katie, these cookies are amazing," Eliza is fawning, closing her eyes in delight. "You have to share your recipe! Aren't they to die for, Mike?"

Mike nods. "They're really good."

"It's just the recipe on the back of the chocolate chip bag," I tell her.

"No way!" she gasps. "I've made that recipe a million times and it never comes out like this."

"That's a true statement," says Mike, finishing his cookie. "Back to work. We have to return the truck by six."

"Okay. It was really nice meeting you, Katie." Eliza reaches for both of my hands and her green eyes grin into mine. "I think we are going to be good friends." Then she's hopping back up into the truck and they are back to work.

I waver about offering to help but I'm not sure how much help I'll be. So I smile at their backs and walk back across the street to my house which smells like Nestle heaven.

I clean up the cookie mess, put the remaining cookies in a plastic bag and I'm in bed with the lights off by seven.

CHAPTER *Four*

I never know what to wear to weddings.

I'm standing in my closet wearing only my underwear, staring at all of my clothes. Black always seems classy but then there's the whole thing about people being in mourning while wearing black and considering I don't even know these people, I can't really be in mourning about their marriage. I've heard you shouldn't wear red and it's like the sin that gets you kicked out of heaven to wear white.

So that basically leaves a bunch of colors that I don't own any dresses in.

And what if this is a casual wedding and everyone there is not going to be super dressy? Or maybe it's a super dressy wedding and I need a floor length gown.

I close my eyes and rub my forehead. Why did I agree to go to this?

Oh wait, I know why. It's because Gram was sitting there all sad and despondent about letting down either of these commitments she'd made and I finally just caved because that's what I do. The word "fine" had barely made it onto my lips before Gram was grinning ear to ear and smashing a silver-wrapped gift with "Kevin and Lisa" written on the card taped to the front into my hands.

I end up pulling on a sleeveless, knee-length black dress and grabbing a nice jacket to wear on top if it gets too cool in the church. Black is classy. That's what I'm going with.

I slide into my heels, transfer my stuff into my nice purse and then I head out to the garage and climb into my car, setting my purse on top of the gift in the passenger seat. Eliza is in front of her house watering the dead flowers in the flower bed under the front window. She's been out there the last two days watering and I haven't had the heart to tell her that she is probably wasting her time. Those flowers were long gone when I moved in six weeks ago and even if by some miracle she brings them back to life, they'll definitely die when a good frost hits in a few weeks.

She waves and I wave and drive down to the main road through town.

Suddenly I realize that though I have the gift, I don't have the invitation and I can't for the life of me remember whether they were getting married at First Presbyterian or First Methodist. I remember Gram told me it was right off the main street, but both of those churches are also right off the main street.

"Gram," I mutter and stop at a red light, digging for my cell phone. I punch her name on the screen and it rings four times.

"Hello," a computerized voice says. "No one is available to take your call. Please leave a message after the tone." *Beep!*

"Gram, it's me. Where is the wedding?"

I click the phone and try calling her again but she again doesn't answer.

Well, maybe I just drive to one of the churches and see if there are a lot of cars out front. It's Saturday at two in the afternoon. Surely a church wouldn't be crowded without a wedding there, right?

I drive down the street and First Presbyterian is on my right. The parking lot is packed and there's an incredible blue 1966 Mustang, if I'm not mistaken, parked out front of the church with the top down and white and cream balloons waving out the back.

Surely this is the church.

I pull into the parking lot and eye the car again. Wow. Dad would have died. Dad was a big old car fanatic and because of that, I know a lot more about cars than I will probably ever need or want to know.

I park, grab the gift and hurry inside. The wedding starts at two and it's about three minutes until then. Just enough time to stick the gift in the pile, sign the guest book for Gram and slide into the back row without having to answer a bunch of "so how do you know the bride or groom?" from the people in the row beside me.

So this will just work out.

I open the doors and there is quiet music in the background, most people have taken their seats. A red-haired man in a tuxedo is standing in front of the double doors that likely lead to the sanctuary.

"Hi," I say.

"Hi," he says in an almost-whisper.

"I'm a little late," I say.

He nods. "The family is just about to walk in."

I find the pen for the guest book and sign it extra quickly. *Kevin and Lisa - prayers for your marriage. –Mabel Laughlin and Katie McCoy*

There's a table overflowing with presents to the right of the guest book and I stick Gram's box precariously on top of a tissue-stuffed bag that is also balanced on top of three other gifts. These people are getting quite a few things. You'd think more men would see this and actually want to get married.

The usher opens the door for me, handing me a program and I slide as quickly as possible into the last row. There's a family with two little girls sitting next to me and we do the whole nod and half smile thing. The woman is already teary.

The music changes right then and the doors open again and the family gets escorted in. Grandparents first and then the mothers. Both of the moms are wearing black and one is visibly holding in tears, patting her face with a black lace hanky. This causes the woman next to me to break down.

Maybe this is a sad wedding. Maybe Kevin and Lisa don't actually belong together. Maybe it's all *Serendipity*-ish of them and one of them has a soul mate on the other side of the world or in New York City, since that's where they always are, waiting for their real love to meet them on top of the Empire State Building.

I watch too many movies.

The moms go up on the stage and attempt to light two candles that I assume will then be both used to light a unity candle, since that seems to be a popular thing to do at weddings.

I look at the program in my lap while the lady I think is the groom's mother has trouble getting her lighter to work.

This happy day is scrolled along the top of the program. Then there's the customary embossed flower in the wedding colors, which look like periwinkle blue and cream.

Underneath the flower, there's more wording.

Tim and Haley, October 24th.

I just blink at the words.

Tim and Haley.

Tim and Haley.

Tim and Haley?

And apparently, the odds can be good that there would be more than one wedding in this small town on this Saturday at two o'clock.

Shoot. I'm scrambling. Maybe I can duck out of here and make it to the other wedding in time. And steal back Gram's gift. It's an engraved casserole dish that she'd had made and I'm pretty sure it says "From the kitchen of Kevin and Lisa Cleary" on it.

Oh boy.

I huff my breath out and I'm about to stand up when the groom and all his groomsmen come in and stand in the front of the church and the music changes yet again and a bridesmaid in possibly the ugliest dress I've ever seen comes swishing right past my elbow.

Oh boy.

One, two, three, four...there are eleven bridesmaids and by the time they all make it through the doors, I'm convinced that there aren't enough bridesmaids in town for the other wedding to have some, too.

Next, two tiny flower girls and a shy looking ring bearer walk down the aisle, all of whom cause the audience to make all kinds of "aww" sounds and giggles.

And then here's the bride. I stand with the rest of the audience as the bridal march begins and wonder if there's a way that I could just duck out into the hallway as soon as she passes me. I mean, no one is going to be looking this way, right?

I am just about to step out when I see the photographer at the end of the aisle by the stage, snapping away and I quickly scoot back into the row. And maybe not.

"We are gathered here together today for the marriage of Tim and Haley," the pastor begins and I sit with the crowd and accept my fate.

Oh boy.

The wedding is long. So, so long. And I don't know if it's because I'm constantly looking at my watch or if it's because they had four special music presentations and did one of those awkward "take home gifts" that supposedly symbolized their unity other than a candle. As far as I can tell, this couple is getting married in a church but it doesn't seem like they are Christians.

And in a weird twist, rather than making one of those sand-in-the-bottle things, this particular couple made a batch of chocolate chip cookie dough, while the pastor narrated.

"And the brown sugar and it's carmelization effect represents how the couple's love for each other will continue to grow strong even with the heat of the world around them."

I assumed this referred to summers in Missouri. I've heard the humidity can be deadly.

Maybe Tim or Haley is a baker or something.

The wedding finally ends, the couple runs down the aisle to applause, the moms come back up the aisle still crying and I'm the first person out the door.

I run to the gift table and Gram's gift is still on top. Maybe I can just swipe it really fast and make a break for First Methodist. I bet if I hurry, I can still have time to sign the other guest book and slide the gift in over there.

I make a grab for the gift and right then I hear, "Hey, what are you doing?"

It's the red-haired usher and he's giving me the stink-eye.

"No, really, it's okay," I whisper quickly as more people are flooding out of the sanctuary. "This is the gift I put here and I realized after the wedding started that I'm at the wrong church."

"I'm sorry?"

"I'm at the wrong church. This is the wrong couple getting married." I yank my gift off and show him the card written in my grandmother's scrawl.

Kevin and Lisa.

"Kevin and Lisa?" the usher frowns.

"Exactly. I'm at the wrong church," I say again.

He just looks at me. People are crowding around us, laughing, brushing tears, comforting the still distraught mothers. The usher finally sighs and nods. "Okay, go ahead and take it."

"Thank you." I grab the box and run for the door. I'm in the car driving down the road only a few minutes later. This wedding was so long thanks to the cookie making session, that I seriously doubt that Kevin and Lisa are actually still at the church.

First Methodist is just down the street and I pull into the parking lot as a line of cars are waiting to get out.

Well, maybe the gifts haven't been taken yet. I have no intention of going to the reception, despite Gram's lecture about the wasted food since she RSVP'd.

I park, grab the gift and run inside to a completely empty foyer.

"Oh man," I mutter.

"Everything okay?" There's a janitor standing in the hallway next to a gigantic trash can. He's busy pulling down decorations from the doorframes.

"Did the wedding party already leave?"

"Yes ma'am. You just missed them. Though I think I heard someone mention that the reception was at the Biltmore Room?"

"Right," I sigh. And it looks like I'm going to the reception. I know my Gram. If I don't deliver this gift and sign the guest book, it's going to be bad news bears for me and my weekly dinners.

I turn back around and follow the last few cars out of the church parking lot and down a few streets to the Biltmore Room.

The Biltmore Room is actually a hotel. It's huge. It has a massive ballroom with a waterfall feature, a five-star restaurant and a few guest rooms. I've never been inside this place, but I've heard the stories.

I follow the crowd in and tell the man at the door my grandmother's name, since I don't have her invitation. It's all dark inside and lit only by the million candles and twinkle lights everywhere. There's a live band on the stage playing songs that Michael Buble made famous again and a dance floor.

Lovely. Because there's nothing like coming to a wedding by yourself to make you hope for a good dance floor.

The man checks the list and then hands me a number. "Table twelve," he tells me and then turns to the people behind me.

I finally spot the gift table and I run the package over. The guest book is open on the table as well and I sign it with the same message.

Okay. Now I can leave.

"Ladies and gentlemen, if you could kindly take your seats, we are about to introduce the bride and groom for the first time," the tuxedo-ed leader of the band says silkily into the microphone.

Everyone who is milling around starts finding their spot and I look anxiously at the door. I can see the bride and groom standing there and it just doesn't seem like a great time to leave.

I'll go after the salad course.

I find Table 12 and sit next to an older woman and her also old husband. "Hello dear," she smiles at me.

"Hi."

Another older lady sits on the other side of me, sliding her cane beside her chair and patting my arm. "Watch if you get out, sweetie. My cane is there," she says.

"Thanks, I'll watch out for it."

"And now, if you could please give a warm welcome for the very first time to Mr. and Mrs. Kevin and Lisa Cleary!" the leader of the band says from where he now sits at a piano and the band bursts into song as the people all applaud and the bride and groom hurry in, going straight to the dance floor and dancing their first dance.

My table is right by the dance floor and as the photographers rush around like they are capturing Brad Pitt and Jennifer Aniston back together again, I realize that I am going to be in like every single picture of their first dance.

Fabulous.

"So, sweetie, how do you know the bride and groom?" the lady with the cane asks me as we watch them swirl around the dance floor.

"Oh, I don't," I say, shaking my head. "I'm actually just here because my grandmother couldn't make it."

"Who is your grandmother, honey?" the other old lady asks, apparently listening to our conversation.

"Mabel Laughlin," I say and both of the old women just start grinning.

"So *you're* Katie," the one with the cane says.

"This make so much more sense now," the other lady smirks.

"What makes sense?" I ask.

"I'm Olive Klein," the lady with the cane says. "That's Frieda Wilder and her husband, Loren."

"Nice to meet you," I say to all of them.

Loren is busy watching the dance but Frieda waves a hand at him. "He's basically lost all of his hearing," she tells me. "And the stubborn oaf won't wear his hearing aids."

"What was that?" Loren asks.

Frieda sighs.

"We've known your grandmother for years," Olive says.

"At least thirty," Frieda nods.

"Probably closer to forty," Olive says. "Anyway, it's a pleasure to meet you, my dear. We've heard a lot about you over the past thirty years."

There's always something weird about meeting someone who knows all about you and you know nothing about them. The song finishes, the bride and groom kiss and everyone applauds as they go to their seats at the head table. Then the bustle of everyone talking and silverware clinking starts up.

"So, what's Mabel up to tonight?" Frieda asks me. "Couldn't handle the steak and lobster? She was always more of a chicken person."

"She had a fundraiser or something at church," I tell them.

"What fundraiser? We don't have a fundraiser today," Frieda says.

I shake my head. "I'm not sure."

"I help the church secretary make the events page and I can tell you for a fact that we do not have any fundraisers today," Olive adds.

I frown. "So why am I here?"

Frieda pats my hand. "Honey, I have no idea. But after forty-ish years of friendship with Mabel Laughlin, I've learned it's just better not to ask. Just accept your fate and whatever comes with it."

"Salad?" There is suddenly a waiter behind us with a tray full of the most gourmet salads I've seen outside of New York. Frieda squeezes my hand and leans back.

"Yes, please. See, honey? Tonight's fate includes this delicious salad."

The waiter sets the salad in front of me and it's already dressed in some sort of citrus-y vinaigrette.

"And let's hear from the father of the bride," the band leader says in his deep, Frank Sinatra voice into the microphone.

A graying man in a tux steps onto the stage and reaches for a microphone. "Claire and I just want to say a warm welcome to all of you and we just want to thank you for the impact you have had on our daughter and our new son. We are so thankful to be here tonight celebrating this lovely couple. And now I'm going to bless the food so we can all eat."

He prays, everyone murmurs amen when he finishes and then digs into the salads.

I crunch a sugar-glazed pecan. The salad is pretty much incredible. There used to be this little lunch place that I would go to sometimes in New York and they served a salad somewhat similar to this one. It was one of my favorite lunches. A big plate of salad and a large iced tea. Though, in New York, there was never the option for sweet tea.

Another reason that Missouri won out when I was considering where to move.

I wonder if I can come to this hotel just to eat lunch.

The band is playing old classics quietly as we eat and it's actually really nice.

"So, Katie, Mabel tells us you just moved from New York," Olive says.

I nod.

"And that you are still unmarried," Frieda adds in.

"Well, that wasn't necessary," Olive says, right as I open my mouth.

"Sure it was. I'm just repeating the facts. She just moved to town and she's unmarried."

"Yes, but I already know the facts and I guarantee that Katie knows that facts. So why do we need to wave them around in front of her? At a wedding?" Olive hisses.

"You waved around a fact."

"I opened up a conversation."

"Well, I did too. Why haven't you gotten married, Katie?" Frieda says.

"Oh Frieda," Olive groans, covering her eyes with a hand.

"It's fine, it's fine," I say, trying to be the peacemaker. I am in the middle of these two women, after all. Might as well try to stop the argument before it turns into something that draws a lot of attention. Based on what I've seen of the feisty Frieda and considering her basically deaf husband, I would imagine that volume control isn't necessarily her strong point.

She's looking at me like she's waiting for me to answer something. I think back to what she asked and sigh.

"You don't have to answer, honey," Olive says.

"It's okay. I haven't gotten married because I just haven't met the right guy yet," I tell Frieda. An obvious answer to the question, but pretty much the correct answer too.

She waves a hand. "Psh. You people these days way overthink things. Why, when Loren and I were young and way more attractive, we weren't so focused on jobs and careers to miss out on the early days of matrimony."

"Priorities are different now," Olive says gently.

I nod. Though, it's not necessarily my priorities that are the problem.

I heard this whole sermon one time about how the biggest problem with modern culture was women in the workforce. Supposedly, it upset the family balance and also led to an increase number of workplace affairs.

I guess I can kind of see the point, but what is a single woman in her thirties supposed to do if she doesn't have a job? Sit at home and crochet? As talented as I am at making a bunch of knots in a string of yarn, I'm just not sure that's the right answer either.

That being said, if I met the right guy and his job was going to relocate him and require me to quit my job or whatever, I would have already quit before the sentence would be completely out of his mouth. I would much rather be married

than be an editor right now. Though, my thought in going into this career was that it would be an ideal one to have when I got married and had kids someday because I could work from home.

Now, though, "when" is looking more like "if".

Weddings just bring out the best conversations.

Time to go.

"Here, let me take that for you," the waiter suddenly appears again and snatches my salad plate from my hands, as I try to stand. I cling on to the plate, trying to hold onto my excuse of looking for the kitchen to put my plate away but finally let it go and sink back to my chair as a plate full of lobster tail, steak, mashed potatoes and grilled asparagus is set in front of me. There's even a little lemon wedge wearing what looks like a shower cap made for rats on the plate.

"What in the world is this?" Frieda asks, poking at the mesh.

"I think it's supposed to keep the seeds from getting on the lobster," I tell her.

"Dear Lord, we can't just pick them off?"

I shrug and squeeze the lemon over the tail. I might as well eat the lobster. I can't even remember the last time I had lobster. Though, the taste is more bitter than I remember. Maybe that's from the conversation.

"Well, I'm just saying, I think your generation has their priorities mixed up."

"Leave the poor girl alone, Frieda," Olive says. "So, Katie, what do you do for a living?"

"I'm an editor," I say. I tell them a little about my job.

"That sounds interesting," Olive says. "I love to read. What a privilege to do that for a job!"

"Hey, there are a bunch of young men here who are pretty attractive," Frieda says, nudging my elbow. "Maybe you should see if one of them wants to dance."

"Frieda, no one else is dancing," Olive says.

"She can start it up."

"I think the band has to open the dance floor," I tell Frieda. Not that I have any intention of asking anyone to dance anyway. I look over at the head table. There is a groomsman who appears to be by himself and is semi-cute, but I'm a firm believer in the man doing the asking. If he wants to dance, he'll come ask.

Based on the way he's staring at his cell phone though, I'm doubting that he has dancing on his mind.

This is the problem with being a woman in today's culture. The men aren't man enough to stop watching their phones or video games or computer screens to just ask us out and see where it goes and I'm just not the type of girl to ask someone out myself.

Basically it equals being thirty-one, alone and stuck between two old women at a wedding talking about careers instead of having a couple of kids and a minivan and talking about diaper brands and educational toys.

Frieda is backing to *psh*-ing. "The band has to open the dance floor? It's not roped off or anything! And the couple already did their first dance."

I nod. "It's just tradition, I think." By this point, I am so done with this wedding. No thanks to Frieda. And what was the deal with Gram making me come here when she really didn't have to miss the wedding?

"All right, ladies and gentlemen, I see that quite a few of you are finishing up your meals, so I'm going to get things rolling. First up, we've got the bride and her father dancing the traditional Father Daughter dance." The band leader is now holding a trumpet and he and a few other members of the band burst out into "My Girl" as the bride and her dad take the floor. Next, we listen to a semi-creepy rendition of "Only You" for the Mother Son dance, but I think that is more the fault of the weeping mother of the groom than the band. The leader keeps sending glances their way as he fluidly plays the piano again, trying to at least make them look like they are keeping the beat and the poor groom has no idea what to do with his mother.

Maybe she doesn't like her new daughter-in-law. Or maybe the daughter-in-law doesn't like her. Either one would be a tricky situation.

I'm heading out as soon as they clear the dance floor. Mostly because it seems rude to leave in the middle of the dance.

The groom finally escorts his sobbing mother back to her chair and takes his spot at the head table again as everyone claps politely. The poor band guy takes the microphone again. "And now, we would like to open the dance floor. We are always up for requests, so please be sure to stop by and let us know what you'd like to hear!" They start up a happy rendition of "Come Fly With Me", probably to get everyone's thoughts off the mother of the groom and her tears.

Several couples from almost every table get up to go dance and by the time they are starting the second verse, the whole dance floor is packed.

Frieda elbows me. "Now's your chance!" she whispers in my ear. "Look, there are quite a few people still sitting and not dancing!"

And the groomsman she is not-so-subtly shrugging to is still looking at his phone.

"I'm good, thank you though."

"Leave her alone," Olive says at the same time that I respond.

"Fine, fine," Frieda says, holding up her hands. "But you tell your grandmother that I tried, you got it? Come on, Loren. Let's go shake a leg."

"What?"

Frieda just shakes her head and starts mumbling something under her breath, pushing her chair back and nodding to the dance floor.

He grins and pulls a hearing aid from his right hand pants pocket, tucking it into his ear. "Sure thing."

"Now you put it in."

"Eh, this way I avoid all the awkward table conversation." He winks at me and holds a hand out to his wife. "May I?"

"Sure. We should request our song," Frieda says.

"Definitely."

They disappear into the crowd on the dimly lit dance floor and I look at Olive. She has a wedding ring on and she twists it around her finger mindlessly as she watches the dancing. "Your husband," I say, trying to figure out the best way to ask it. "Is he...?"

"Oh honey, Walter died a good twenty years ago," Olive says.

"I'm so sorry to hear that."

"Don't be. He loved the Lord and he was in a great deal of pain for many years before the Lord took him home. He's happy and whole now." She sighs at the dance floor. "But goodness knows I do get lonely at times like these." She shakes her head. "There's just something about going to a wedding alone, you know?"

"I know."

Olive smiles at me and pats my hand with her wrinkled one. "We will just be brave together then, okay?"

I smile back and I just kind of know that this lady is going to be a good friend.

"So about that groomsman," she grins at me and I roll my eyes.

"He hasn't stopped looking at his phone all night," I tell her and she looks over at him, frowning.

"True. Good looks are fine and all but let me tell you, there are plenty of couples that married for looks who are divorced now that they are old like me. Well, someone will come along."

And there's the phrase I hate more than almost any other. But Olive is so nice that I just kind of stifle my groan and nod.

"Katie? Katie, come here!" Frieda is on the edge of the dance floor, holding Loren's hand and motioning me over. She's on the verge of making a scene, so I quickly jump up and hurry over. Maybe Loren lost his hearing aid or something.

"What's wrong?" I ask her.

"Luke asked for requests and he's too high and too loud for us to get close to him," Frieda says. "I even took out Loren's hearing aid and we still couldn't get close to the speakers or those ridiculously loud trumpets. Can you ask him to play 'The Way You look Tonight'?" She dimples. "It's our song."

"Um. Sure." I'm assuming Luke is the band leader. I must have missed his introduction.

Nothing like making a request for a super romantic song and then sitting back down at my table with my eighty-plus year-old new friend.

I make my way around the edge of the dance floor and stand quietly by the corner of the stage until the band finishes "Swing". The crowd applauds, the band leader bows and then notices me standing there and smiles, stepping over to the edge of the stage and bending down.

"Got a request?" he asks, grinning and even though I wouldn't call him super attractive, his voice is so smooth, it's like God created him to be in front of a microphone.

"My friend wants to hear 'The Way You Look Tonight'," I tell him.

"A popular choice. Sure thing!" He nods and stands back up, immediately leading the band into the song. I see Frieda's happy wave as I work my way back around to my table and I smile.

"She's annoying but still kind of loveable, isn't she?" Olive says to me as I sit down.

I just laugh.

CHAPTER *Five*

Sunday morning and I'm back to laying in bed, staring at the ceiling, asking Jesus if I really need to go to church. I mean, I spent the whole afternoon yesterday being social with people I don't know. So, surely that counts right?

I mean, sure, I heard more about how to bake a batch of cookies at the wrong wedding ceremony than I heard an actual sermon, but maybe I could just listen to a Christian radio station in the car or something this week.

I groan and roll out of bed.

Sometimes you don't have to hear a thunder clap or a loud voice from heaven to know what you're supposed to do.

In thirty minutes, I'm out of the shower, I've got my hair blow-dried and messily curled and I'm putting on mascara. I finish my makeup and I've got time to spare before church, so I decide to drive through Starbucks and get myself a latte.

I'm pulling out of the garage and I see Eliza out front of her house, watering again. She is determined to get those dead plants back to life. She's wearing a skirt and a silky shirt and I wonder if she is going somewhere for church as well.

She sees my car and waves and I roll down my window. "Hi Eliza," I say.

"Katie! Great to see you." She steps closer and puts her hands on my open passenger window. "On your way to church?" she asks me.

"Yeah."

"Which one do you go to?"

"The jury is still out on that," I say, shrugging. "I'm trying First Community Church again today."

"Hey, that was on my list too!"

"Want to tag along?" Suddenly the thought of not sitting alone in the back row of the church sounds incredibly wonderful.

She grins at me. "Let me grab my purse and my Bible."

She's back in thirty seconds and she climbs into the car, pulling her seatbelt on with a huge smile. "Oh this is so wonderful!" she says. "I hate going to churches by myself and Mike always worries about me going alone because he thinks that small towns are just a big pool of cults."

"Your brother worries a lot, doesn't he?"

"You don't even know the half of it."

"Want to stop by Starbucks first?"

"See, now you are speaking my language."

I pull up to the drive through window a few minutes later and order us both Pumpkin Spice Lattes. We are driving away and the car is filling up with the sweet, cinnamon-y scent a few minutes later.

"So, have you been to this church before?" Eliza asks me, sipping her coffee.

"I went last week."

"Well, that's a good sign that you're willing to go back!"

I nod. "I think this is actually the first one that I'll have gone to twice."

"So, Katie, you just moved here too, right?"

I nod again. "Yeah, about two months ago."

"Isn't it just the cutest little town? I had Thursday and Friday off this week, so I walked down by the river and then spent one day downtown. Have you eaten at that little old fashioned ice cream parlor yet?"

I shake my head. "I haven't been downtown yet."

"Oh my gosh, Katie, we have got to go together! There are the cutest little shops and a gazebo that overlooks the river and this huge park right in the middle that has a big open-sided barn on it that they use for square dancing in the summers! I met like thirty people who were just so kind and welcoming. It's just about the most adorable little downtown on the planet. I think you will love it."

"It sounds cute." And sort of weird, small-town-ish. I'm used to New York and it's very noncommittal ways, unless we are discussing your relationship to your work. Then there needs to be commitment and more than one hundred percent of it.

"Do you square dance?" she asks.

"I never have. Do you?"

"No, and honestly, I'm not entirely sure what that even is. Is it dancing in a square? Or do you step in the shape of a square? Or maybe you have a partner and you have to hold hands and make a square with your arms?"

I shrug. "I guess it could be any of those things." We pull into the church parking lot and Eliza gasps.

"This is the biggest church I have seen outside of St. Louis!"

"I know, right? Here, don't forget your Bible."

"Thanks."

We walk inside, nodding to the greeter and I am heading for the back row, but Eliza just keeps marching up the aisle toward the closer rows.

I just stand there for a minute because I'm not really the yelling in church type but I also really do not want to sit in the front rows. What if the pastor spits when he preaches? What if the front rows have already been claimed by people? What if it's like at a baseball game and the close seats are handed down through the generations?

"Hey, Katie, here's a couple of seats right here!" Eliza waves at me.

Well, now I have to go. A bunch of people are looking now. I smile sort of sheepishly at them and hurry down the aisle as quickly as I can without bringing more attention to ourselves.

Eliza plops down in the middle of the row so there will be absolutely no chance for escape once a few more people show up and takes a long drink of her latte.

"What a beautiful sanctuary!" she says, and I'm beginning to think that the girl has no form of volume control. She is just either loud or louder but nothing softer than that. Meanwhile, I tend to operate in a quieter tone of voice and mind.

I wonder how her patients do with all the yelling?

"Tell me more about your job," I say in a very soft voice, hoping she'll get the hint and drop a few decibels.

"I work in the postpartum ward," she says just as loud as ever.

You would think she would need to be quieter with all those sleeping, newborn babies in there.

"Do you like it?"

"I love it. Love it. There's just something really special about getting to know someone right after such a huge life event. And I mean, my favorites are the new parents. They are just adorable. And people have asked me how I handle the crying, but the screaming babies start to kind of fade into the background the longer you're there and really, even the mom's tears are just pretty common now. You just have to speak loudly over the babies and give lots of hugs to the mamas."

Thus the volume, I guess.

She grins at me and it's such a sweet, totally innocent smile that I have to smile back.

I barely know Eliza, but I imagine she's one of the best nurses in the hospital.

She nudges my shoulder with hers. "I think we are going to be great friends, Katie," she says as the band comes to the stage.

A tiny glimmer of something really strange and warm glows in my stomach and I can't help the smile.

I think so too.

Monday morning I'm up, dressed and dutifully turning on my computer, a cup of hot coffee beside me. I spent the day yesterday helping Eliza rip out all the dead flowers in her front yard and plant some fall mums, both in her front yard and in a few pots on my front porch, thanks to her insistence.

I glance out the window and I can see the dark cranberry mums on the table out there and I smile.

It does sort of season up the place.

I start with my emails, answer a bunch of questions from Joe and then get to work on the romantic mystery. This is getting worse by the chapter. I'm a fan of romance novels but there's a limit to the gushiness. Plus, I feel like this couple in the book has absolutely no chemistry. It's totally all about the kissing and how his breath always smells like sweet coffee.

I'm sorry, but has this author smelled coffee breath before? It's not an attractive thing. I remember Joe drinking coffee by the trough-full when I lived in New York. He even had a personal coffeemaker on his desk and the thing was refilling a gigantic twelve-cup pot every hour or so. The man's insides had to have reached new levels of acidity known to man. Anyway, he would come in my office and vent about some author or another editor and I would just hand him an Altoid before he even got all the way in the door.

I like coffee but not enough that I think coffee breath is sexy.

I'm making good progress at lunch time so I decide to work through lunch and take the laptop to Panera. The day is overcast and a little on the chilly side. Fall is officially here and it's time for some broccoli cheese soup in a bread bowl. And maybe a pumpkin scone, since it has been proven that carbs are linked to high productivity. Or maybe I'm just making that statistic up.

I drive to Panera, find a table near the fireplace, plop my stuff down to save it and go stand in line with my wallet.

Working from home can be lonely, so it's nice to be out in the general public. I look around and there is a wide assortment of people here. Moms with their kids meeting other moms with their own children, business lunches, a couple of elderly women talking over soups and salads. There are even a few tables like me, one person with a laptop. It looks sort of sad considering the conversations flooding around them.

"Can I help the next in line?" the cashier says, looking right at me.

I order my soup and a scone and take my number to my table. By the time I get connected to the wifi and email a reply to Joe again, my soup and scone are here and the smells are making my mouth water.

The soup is perfect and I half work and half watch the line to order get longer and longer until it's out the door. Ninety percent of the people who sit down have a bowl of steaming soup in front of them. Apparently, I am not the only person who listened to the call of the weather.

"Excuse me, are you using the outlet?"

I look up and I totally recognize the voice but I cannot place the person in front of me anywhere. He's wearing slim cut jeans, a red plaid button down shirt and glasses and his dark hair is all curly and messy on his head.

"Nope, go ahead," I say, nodding to the wall. He plugs in his computer cord and nods to me.

"Thanks so much."

"Yeah, no problem." Now it's just bugging me. Maybe he goes to First Community and I saw him in the hallways. Or maybe he works over at the senior center where Gram lives? There are quite a few guys around my age who work there. And it's not like I meet a bunch of men all over town.

But I swear I have heard his voice before.

I try to surreptitiously glance over at him as I'm taking a bite of my soup. He doesn't really look like one of the maintenance guys I've seen at the center. Plus, Gram knows all of them by name and so I know most of them now, too. This guy next to me isn't wearing a ring. I think only one of the four guys is still single and there's a good reason for it. He's got an interesting personality.

The man is busy typing away on his computer, a deli sandwich and a fizzing Coke on the table next to him. Maybe he didn't get the memo about it being fall and time for soups.

"Sorry, are you sure I'm not in your way with the cord?" he asks, suddenly looking up at me and I totally flush with color, realizing that I was just staring at him with my brow all furrowed while I was trying to figure out where I knew him.

"Oh goodness, no. I'm sorry." I rub my red cheeks like maybe that will make them simmer down, but I'm pretty sure it just makes them more red. "I'm sorry, I just feel like I've met you somewhere and I can't figure out where."

He just kind of looks at me.

Great.

If possible, I'm now blushing even more because I just realize that I have said the oldest line in the entire book.

I cover my face with my hands. "I'm sorry. I just...I'm sorry." I wish I was done eating so I could just leave and be saved any more embarrassment.

I reach for my spoon but now my hands are all shaky because my nerves are just shot at this point.

And now we can see why I'm still single. I close my eyes and pray for a little bit of respite here. *Seriously, Jesus, can You just poof him to a different table or something?* I'm not usually like this around men but this is just awkward.

There is no good way to eat soup when you don't have one hundred percent control over your hands. Soup is dead to me.

I shift my chair a little so my back is more toward the man so I can hopefully just finish my scone and not say anything else dumb.

I don't even care that I've seen him somewhere before. Or heard him. He actually doesn't look familiar at all.

Probably he just sounds like someone I know. Maybe he's a radio host. Maybe he reminds me of someone from New York. Goodness knows you there's never a break in what you hear there. I remember it took me a good month before I was really used to the quiet here.

Joe is on the ball with the email replies. I click over to my mail.

Gagging yet?

I flip back over to Sue's mystery. She's been describing in detail both a murder scene and then a few pages later, a coffee-breath make out session again.

Seriously.

She needs to stick to either romance or crime novels but not both at the same time.

A minute later, my mailbox shows a new message again and it's Joe.

You're telling me. I was the one campaigning against the acquisition.

The problem is that Sue Chariston has written about twenty books for Townsend and Mitchell and almost every single one has become a New York Times bestseller. They would have published a phone book if she'd written it. And Sue knows it. So, of course, she can get away with crappy writing and terrible descriptions. She knows it's going to be published and if only because of her name, she knows she's going to make bank on it.

Yet another reason I like editing up-and-coming authors rather than established bestsellers. They work harder for it.

I finish my scone while managing not to say anything dumb to anyone, including Joe who keeps emailing me. It must be one of those rare slow days at the office. I'm eyeing my soup, wondering if I should attempt to try to eat it again. My hands are pretty steady.

I'll try it.

I pull the plate with the bread bowl on it a little closer and I have the spoon halfway in my mouth when I hear, "Excuse me, I need to get to that cord again."

I manage to swallow the soup and actually set my spoon down. I turn to the man and nod. "Okay." I am not anywhere close to the cord since I moved my chair around a little bit.

"I just didn't want you to think I was sneaking up behind you," he says.

"Okay," I say again because I'm not sure what else to say. He stands up, unplugs the cord and wiggles the end around a little bit.

"I'm having trouble with the charger," he says.

"Sorry about that."

"Yeah, it's really annoying. Especially when I have work to do." He looks up at me through his glasses. "Are you working, too?"

I nod. "Yes."

"Cool. What do you do?"

I'm trying to see this as friendly conversation instead of getting creeped out. Sometimes I hate this world that we live in and what it has done to women and their sense of safety. And it doesn't help that my Gram is constantly emailing me the most terrifying stories of new ways that serial killers try to lure in their victims.

The last one included a man saying he needed help because his baby was locked in the car.

We live in a sick, twisted world.

I look at the normal, seemingly nice man in front of me and I try to stick with the bare basics. "I'm an editor."

"For books?"

"Yeah."

"Very cool."

Now it just seems weird not to ask him what he does. "So what do you do?" I ask after a pause.

"Oh, I do a bunch of things," he says.

Maybe that's code for he doesn't have a job. Or a steady one, anyway. Isn't that what they always say? I met a guy one time in a coffee shop in New York who cleaned koi ponds for a living. I don't know anyone in New York who owns a koi pond.

Come to think of it, I don't know anyone period who owns a koi pond.

The guy said business was slow.

The man adjusts his glasses. "Right now I'm working as a consultant for an engineering firm outside of Dallas," he says. "I have to travel there a lot, but thankfully I don't have to move there. Unlike the other inhabitants of Texas, I actually like to enjoy all four seasons."

I smile. I've never lived in Texas but I've heard the stories.

"That's neat," I say.

"Yeah. It's only a two year contract, but I'll probably get pulled into at least another year, if not two. And on the side, I do weddings."

I just look at him. "Like you plan them?" I ask.

"I perform at them."

The light goes off. "*That's* where I know you from!" I exclaim, much louder than I mean to be. He grins.

"I thought you looked familiar, too. You were at the wedding last weekend, right? Sitting at the table off to the side? I think you even requested a song."

I nod. "That was me."

"'The Way You Look Tonight'?"

I can feel my eyebrows going up. Either he's got a really good memory or I'm back to square one with the serial killer theory.

He nods. "I get a lot of requests for that song, but not usually from someone so young. It got stuck in my memory."

"It was for an older couple who was also at my table."

"I figured when I didn't see you out on the dance floor. That's my grandparents' favorite song."

"So how long have you been doing the wedding thing?" I ask.

He shrugs and angles his chair a little bit so he's not twisting weird to talk to me. "About four years, maybe? It's actually starting to make almost as much as my contracting jobs, but I don't feel like it's really a grown-up job, so I just keep doing both. Plus, it's primarily on the weekends and I keep up the contracting because I need something to do during the week. I don't sit well."

I nod because I understand what he means. Even though my whole job is sitting down, I just don't like to be bored. I end up sleeping all the time or binge watching shows on Netflix which doesn't do anyone any good.

He plugs his computer cord back in. "I'm Luke, by the way." He digs in his pocket, pulls out a wallet and hands me a card.

Luke Brantley.

Sounds like a country singer. There's a picture of him on the card with his hair all slicked down, wearing a tux and holding a microphone, exactly how he looked at the wedding last weekend. I look over at him now and while I can see some similarities with the jawline, he looks totally different right now.

No wonder I didn't recognize him.

Making your event special!

The man obviously needs some help with his cards, but I would imagine his business is more word of mouth than anything else right now.

"What's your name?" he asks me.

I look at the card and then back at him. I mean, he did sing at a friend of Gram's wedding. And I know that Gram knew the girl's parents or something from her church. So, if they could trust that he wasn't some sort of weirdo, maybe I can, too.

"Katie," I say, sticking with just the first name.

"Nice to meet you, Katie. Do you come to Panera often?"

"Not often," I say. Almost weekly isn't exactly often, is it? And it's not like I come every single Monday for lunch. Just occasionally and especially when it's overcast and cooler.

Meaning I'll be here a lot more in the near future with winter approaching, but I don't tell him this.

Time to head out before the questions start getting a little more personal.

"Well, my working lunch is over," I say to him.

"You didn't eat the bread bowl," he says, nodding to my table.

"I ate the inside."

"The crust is the best part."

I hand him my plate. "Help yourself."

He grins. "Thanks."

I close my laptop, put it in the case, zip it up and turn to Luke Brantley, who really should have been a country singer with that name, despite his silky oldies voice.

"Nice to meet you, Luke."

"Nice to meet you, Katie." He grins at me behind those glasses. "I hope we run into each other again. And if you ever need a wedding singer, you know who to call."

I pause on my way out. "Do you ever sing country?"

"No. Do you like country?"

I shrug. "When it's not about trucks or one night stands."

He smirks. "Then I'd say you probably don't like country."

I grin and take my exit.

I climb into my car, lock the doors, toss my laptop on the passenger seat and start the ignition.

Well. That was interesting.

CHAPTER *Six*

"So. What are you doing for dinner tonight?"

I look at the weird number on the phone and try to place the girl's voice on the other end. I know this voice, I just don't have the number programmed into my cell, apparently.

"I'm sorry?"

"Katie?"

"Yeah?"

"It's Eliza."

Ah-ha. "Oh hi."

"Do you have dinner plans?"

I snort. "Do I ever have dinner plans?"

"I sense some bitterness."

"Not bitterness. Just..." Actually, maybe bitterness was the right word, but saying it out loud just sounds so...so...

Well, bitter. It's not a word that a good Christian girl is supposed to have as part of her description.

"Well, you have plans tonight," Eliza declares. "We are going bowling."

"I'm sorry?"

"Bowling? You know, that sport where you chuck a shiny, marbled-looking ball down a very slick runway and it crashes into a bunch of white things that look like a weird play on a turkey leg?"

I grin. "I know what bowling is, Eliza. Though, I've never heard it described like that before."

"They do look like turkey legs."

Now that I'm thinking about it, I can kind of see it. "Why do you want to go bowling?"

"Because I was driving home from grocery shopping today and I saw a bowling alley. I haven't been bowling since I was twelve years old at Ashley Kaseman's birthday party and I remember it being kind of fun. They are having a Monday night special for pizza and two rounds of bowling for ten dollars and that sounds like a good deal to me."

"Okay," I say slowly. "I mean, I don't have any other plans."

"Great! It's the You-Can-Bowl close to downtown. You can ride with me, if you want."

"Sure."

"Great!" she exclaims again. "I'll see you at six."

"Okay."

I hang up and spend the rest of the afternoon working and doing a few loads of laundry. At five-thirty, I change back into the jeans and striped shirt I wore to Panera earlier. I never wear jeans if I'm going to be at home. I am always back into my pajamas pants within three minutes of getting home.

I attempt to make my hair a little less on the wild side and walk out front, pocketing my front door key after I lock the door.

Eliza is standing by her car, waving, sunglasses on her face and grinning at me. "Hey neighbor!" she shouts across the street.

I wave and walk over. "Hey," I say, not nearly as loud.

"Ready for a rousing evening full of haphazardly knocking things over?" she asks me, grinning.

"Sure," I say.

"Well, let's do it!"

I climb in the car and she chats the whole way to the bowling alley about her new job and how much she is liking it. "I mean, it's just the cutest hospital. And we seriously have some amazing nurses on our staff. I'm just so blessed to have gotten a job here!"

"That's great, Eliza."

"How is your job going? Did you finish the book?"

I shake my head. I have another three chapters in the initial edit and then I have to complete the line edit, where you go through the book one word at a time.

I'm already dreading that one.

"Not quite," I tell her.

"Lots of corrections?"

I rub my head. "You don't even want to know."

"Sorry about that."

"It's fine. It's all part of the job. I'm sure there are parts of your job that I'd rather not know about, too."

She grins. "Where do I start?"

"Please don't."

She laughs.

We pull into the parking lot and there are quite a few cars there. Apparently, the ten dollar deal they have is a popular one. We wait in line in the entrance that smells like a weird mix of spray deodorant, stale cigarette smoke and grease. Then a frizzled hair woman at the desk who is chewing a large piece of gum looks at us. "Next!" she barks.

"Two please for the ten dollar thing," Eliza says, handing her a ten dollar bill. I dig out my cash as well.

"What size shoe?"

We tell her our shoe size and she plops two pairs of the absolute ugliest, nastiest looking shoes on the planet on the counter and takes our money. "Lane eight," she says gruffly. "Pepperoni pizza will be available in ten minutes. Next!"

"Ick," Eliza says, using the tips of her fingers to grab the shoes. "These are a health violation."

"No kidding."

"I'm glad I brought my thickest pair of socks," she says.

"I wish I had."

"Sorry, Katie. Hopefully the pizza is good!"

We find our lane and take our cute, clean, good-smelling shoes off and put on the nasty, falling-apart, stinky shoes the lady gave us. There's a group of older men and women in matching teal button down shirts at the lane to our right. When one of them turns their back, I can see *Midtown Mavericks* embroidered on the back of the shirts with a bowling ball right below the words. They are taking turns hitting strike after strike. Half of them aren't even watching the other people bowl, they're just sitting at the tables with the weird, pull out swivel chairs and talking.

Eliza elbows me. "Hey, check out the girl next to us," she says in what is probably as close to as whisper as she can manage.

I look to the left of us. I thought it was an empty lane, but there's a girl sitting at the table, shaking her head forlornly at her cell phone. She's wearing bowling shoes, only hers don't look nearly as nasty. She has on a really cute skirt and a camisole under a mint-colored sweater, like she's holding on to summer colors but still practical enough to know it's getting chilly outside. She rubs a hand through her slightly longer than shoulder-length brown, super curly hair and sighs.

"I wonder if her date isn't coming," Eliza whispers.

"Maybe." I feel weird staring at her in the midst of her obvious sadness.

"She looks really familiar."

She doesn't to me, but based on the morning's events at Panera, I think I've proven my lack of talent when it comes to remembering faces.

Eliza is staring at her, brow furrowed and I elbow her lightly. "Stop it, she's going to see you."

Eliza pops up straight and snaps her fingers. "I know where I saw her! She was sitting down the row from us at First Community yesterday!"

I look at the girl again and I swear I have never seen her a day in my life.

"I don't know, Eliza…"

"It's totally her. I remember thinking her hair was so cool. I've always wanted curly hair. I think it's gorgeous." Eliza runs a hand through her super straight auburn hair and sighs. "Grass is always greener, right? I'm going to go ask her what's wrong."

"She's obviously upset," I say, quietly. "Why don't we just leave her alone? I don't want her to think that everyone is staring at her."

Eliza shrugs. "If she's upset, then she'll need some cheering up. Let's go meet her!" She marches over in her ugly shoes before I can say anything else.

I close my eyes and take a deep breath. Eliza totally and completely pushes me out of my comfort zone. Maybe it's a good thing, but right now it just feels like a total invasion of this poor girl's privacy.

"Hi there," I hear Eliza say and the girl looks up, eyes red-rimmed from holding in tears.

I walk over, trying to be the calm one who leads Eliza back out of what is definitely not her business.

"Hi," the girl sniffs.

"I'm Eliza and this is Katie," Eliza says. "What's your name?"

"Ashten."

"That's a great name!" Eliza exclaims. "Hey, do you go to First Community Church?"

The girl rubs her nose with the back of her hand and nods. "Yeah, I've been there for a couple of months. Do you guys?"

"We just went last week!" Eliza says. "See, I told you, Katie! I totally recognized you. Your hair, actually. It's gorgeous."

"Thanks," Ashten says slowly, raking a hand through it, getting her fingers stuck in the curls and just tucking it behind her ear.

"Anyway, are you here by yourself? Because you should totally have Ms. Frizzle at the desk up there transfer your game over to our lane so we can all play together. Bowling is more fun with more people anyway."

She blinks and swipes under her eyes. "I mean, I guess I can do that. I was supposed to be meeting someone here, but it looks like he isn't coming."

Uh oh. Poor girl. I smile as gently, trying to keep all traces of pity out of it. "You should definitely come play on our lane," I tell her.

She nods. "I'll go talk to the lady. By the way, her name isn't really Ms. Frizzle."

"It should be," Eliza says, shrugging.

Ashten smiles for the first time since we met her and I notice how pretty her brown eyes are. "I'll be right back." She climbs up the five stairs to get to the top level where the desk and food court are and a few minutes later, another spot for another name pops up on the screen suspended above our lane.

"Great!" Eliza says and sits down at the desk to input all of our names.

"How do you spell Ashten?" she asks as Ashten rejoins us, sitting at our table.

She spells her name and then looks at us. "You guys haven't been in Carrington Springs very long, have you?" she asks.

"How did you know?" I ask. I look over at the screen. "It's Katie with a K," I tell Eliza.

"Oh, my bad. I'll fix it."

"Thanks."

"Well, for starters, you guys are both wearing the shoes they rent here. The locals all know to avoid them like the plague."

My feet immediately start itching. "Why?" I ask, trying to hide the terror. I'm instantly envisioning those little puke-green monsters they show climbing under people's toenails in that toenail fungus commercial burrowing into my foot and slithering into my leg.

Eliza looks at her shoe. "It stinks but it didn't look contagious."

"All I know is that you guys should probably take a good shower tonight. And maybe do one of those salt scrub things. Isn't salt supposed to be healthy for you?"

"Not if you eat too much," Eliza says.

She smiles and glances down at her phone again.

"Girl, if he hasn't written you by now, I say you should just forget about him," Eliza says.

Ashten sighs and smiles a forlorn smile at us. "Wish I could. It's my brother, though. He's kind of hard to forget."

Eliza grins. "Hey! I've got one of those, too. An older brother was the best and worst thing I've ever been given."

Ashten laughs. "Exactly. Only mine is younger." Her eyes get all misty and red-rimmed again.

"What do you do?" I ask her, trying to take her mind off her brother and his apparent ability to make her cry.

"I'm a teacher," she says.

"Oh neat! What grade?" I ask.

"Third. I love it." And there is a sweet sparkle that starts to glow in her previously sad eyes. "This is my eighth year teaching and my fourth year with the third grade."

I do some quick calculations and decide she is pretty much right around thirty, like Eliza and I are.

Eliza finishes getting the computer set up and starts doing a few back bends and lunges.

"What are you doing?" Ashten finally asks, since both of us are just staring at her.

"Stretching. I always stretch before I go bowling."

Ashten exchanges a look with me. "When was the last time you went bowling?" I ask Eliza.

"About eight years ago. Why?"

I grin. "Let's play."

The team next to us is still throwing strike after strike. Eliza had put my name in first, so I'm feeling the pressure of over a decade of a bowling-free existence. I pick up the purple-marbled ball which, if I'm being honest, I picked more for the color than the weight. I watch a lady who is probably in her sixties in the lane next to me out of the corner of my eye so I can see what she does.

She holds the ball in both hands in front of her, takes three gigantic steps and then swipes her back leg out behind her and lets the ball go down the lane.

Instant strike.

I take a deep breath and hold the ball in front of me.

"Let's go, Katie, let's go!" Eliza chants behind me.

I take three big steps, plant my right foot, attempt to slide my back foot behind me, but the shoes I'm wearing have lost any sense of slide. The shoe gets stuck halfway there and I can feel myself falling right as I let go of the ball.

I watch from a tangled heap on the floor as my ball sails right into the gutter.

"Oh my gosh!" Eliza yells.

"Are you okay, honey?" the lady asks beside me.

I know my cheeks have to be the same color as the neon "No Smoking" signs hanging up everywhere as I scramble to my feet and wave everyone off. "I'm fine, I'm fine," I say, but my tush is suddenly killing me.

The older I get, the harder something like this hurts.

I walk back to the ball return machine, trying not to emphasize the fact that I am now rubbing the smarting right cheek on my behind.

Eliza is grinning at me like a kid in a hot dog commercial. "So, how long has it been since you've bowled?" she asks and starts laughing.

Ashten is a little more sensitive. "Are you okay?" she asks, but it's obvious by how she's half-covering her mouth that she's trying to hide a smile.

"I'm fine," I say again as my ball pops out of the machine.

"The goal is to knock the pins down, Katie," Eliza says. "Not yourself."

"Oh, that's what the goal is," I say, shaking my head and picking up the ball. I take a deep breath and walk toward the lane again, only this time I don't try to slide my back leg behind me. I just stop in front of the lane, hold the ball and underhand it down the lane. It rolls one way and then the next, taking it's time reaching the pins. Then it knocks two pins down before crazily careening off to the side and landing in the gutter in the back.

"Yay!" Eliza says.

Ashten claps.

I am never coming bowling again.

The pizza is obviously made by the same people who take care of the shoes, so we ditch the pizza idea, finish up our rounds and the three of us head to Chili's for dinner.

I scrub my hands down with the hottest water I can stand and about eight pumps of the sickly sweet smelling soap in the restaurant bathroom. By the time I get back, the waitress is there with her notepad.

I order the Southwestern Egg Rolls and a mango iced tea. I love Chili's, but it's a weird place to come to by yourself. Gram always complains about heartburn when I try to convince her to come here for Friday night dinner, so I never get to come. Ashten orders some kind of a salad and Eliza gets soup, salad and soft pretzel bites that she shares with all of us. We have to order another basket before our other food even comes.

"So. Ashten. Tell us your story," Eliza says.

Ashten loosened up a lot in the bowling alley. I think that's Eliza's doing, though. The girl is a natural at getting people to feel comfortable. I imagine this probably also makes her an amazing nurse.

Ashten smiles. "What do you want to know?"

"Have you always lived here? What made you become a teacher? How long have you loved Jesus? I don't know. The basics," Eliza says.

"Are you dating anyone?" I ask.

"Oo!" Eliza perks up. "Yes, are you?"

Ashten shakes her head. "Nope, completely single over here. And yes, I did grow up here. Actually, my family has a restaurant that my great-grandparents owned."

"No way!" Eliza says.

I grin. "That's cool. Like what kind of food?"

"It's all kinds of food. Mostly like old-time grill style. Hamburgers, sandwiches, soups. My great-grandpa was the master griller, so we're known for our steaks and portion sizes. And our rolls."

Eliza brightens. "Wait, you aren't talking about Minnie's Diner right outside town, are you?"

Ashten nods. "That's the one!"

"Holy cow! That place is amazing! And it's renowned. When I ate there, a group of twenty people came in who had rented a charter bus and driven up from Memphis just for the rolls!"

Ashten nods. "It's pretty well known."

"So do you live outside of town, too?" I ask her. I haven't done too much exploring inside Carrington Springs. I've done absolutely nothing outside of it.

She shakes her head to my question. "No, only in the summer when I'm not teaching. It was just too far of a commute for me to live there full time. In the winter, we always have the possibility of getting a lot of snow, so it was just more practical to live closer to the school. But I go work at the restaurant during the summer months."

"You are the coolest person I've ever met," Eliza declares.

"Thanks," I say, elbowing her.

She grins at me, chomping a soft pretzel bite.

Ashten smiles. "It's different, that's for sure. My shifts at the restaurant in the summer start so early that I usually end up just moving back home during those months. But school is in right now, so right now I'm in town. My brother is going to take the restaurant over from my parents. He basically runs it now."

"Same brother who stood you up?" Eliza asks.

For all her talent at making people feel calm and comfortable, Eliza is the least tactful person I've ever met.

Ashten sighs. "One and the same. He's my only sibling, actually. He's just not the best at communication. He's really busy right now with the restaurant and he met this girl, so I know she is taking priority." Her lips twist a little and she sighs. "I guess I'm just not used to it yet. I mean, I knew it would happen eventually, but I always kind of thought I'd be the first one, you know? I am two years older than him."

Eliza and I are both nodding.

"What about you guys? Are either of you dating anyone? You aren't wearing rings, so I'm assuming not married."

Eliza shakes her head. "I've been so focused on nursing school and then my job that I haven't had much time for anything else. And besides that, I have the opposite issue. My brother is so ridiculously overprotective, I probably wouldn't be allowed to date whoever I met anyway. No one is ever as good as they should be, according to Mike, anyway."

I nod. I could see that.

"Mike is your brother?" Ashten asks.

"Yeah. He lives in St. Louis. That's part of the reason I moved. He's just a huge worrywart. And I mean, I get it. It's just the two of us. My dad died in a car accident when I was in middle school and then my mom died of breast cancer when I was sixteen. So, he was my legal guardian for two years. I know that what happened with my parents has made him way more protective that he probably would have been otherwise. But still. He worries too much."

I had no idea that this was Eliza's story.

They both look at me. I shrug. "I mean, my story is fairly boring compared to yours," I say. "I moved here from New York, but my mom grew up here and my Gram still lives here. So, I see her every Friday night for dinner. I've always wanted to meet someone but..." I shrug because it's too painful to keep talking.

Sometimes I can joke about it and make light of the situation, but honestly, there are a lot of days where I just feel...

Forgotten. Not good enough. Left out.

It's bad enough that I've actually deleted most of my social networking profiles. I just can't look at more wedding and baby pictures from every single person I grew up with. It seems like every day someone is announcing something life changing and I'm just sitting here correcting the work of an overdramatic romance writer who wants to be a suspense author.

Not too much to post on Facebook about that kind of stuff.

I do have friends who are single. Most of them are my New York friends and most of them are so cynical that they look at the idea of marriage from a one hundred and eighty degree different view than I do. Most of the people I worked with came from broken homes and most of them thought lifelong monogamy was a sentence only comparable to life in a high security prison.

My parents have a great marriage, which is probably a big reason why I want to be married, too. I know it hasn't always been easy for them. They got pregnant with me right after their wedding and then tried for a sibling for me over the next eight years before finally just deciding it wasn't in God's plan. I know those years were tough. I remember going with Mom to doctor's appointments and she had a couple of surgeries throughout the years.

Then the twins sort of fell into their lap and we all knew it was what was supposed to happen. But it hasn't been easy on them. Twins are rough. And Mom and Dad aren't in their twenties anymore. But they are still some of the most loving, sacrificial people I know.

Eliza and Ashten are just looking at me and I shrug, blinking back to the present. "Anyway, that's me," I say.

"And you're an editor," Eliza says.

"Right."

"Have you ever been close to getting married?" Ashten asks.

I shake my head. "I've never even been on more than two dates with the same person," I say.

"What about you?" Eliza asks Ashten.

She shrugs. "A few years ago, I met a guy who I thought was the one. We dated for six months and right when things were starting to get semi-serious, he moved to Anchorage."

"As in Alaska?"

"One and the same," Ashten nods.

"Wow. So I'm assuming that kind of ended things," Eliza says.

She nods. "We weren't at the place where I would have considered moving with him and I certainly wasn't going to go unless we were already married. It seemed silly to quit my job here and try to find a job and an apartment there while living in a city where I knew one person and was fifty thousand miles away from anyone else I'd ever known just for the possibility of him being the right one." She shrugs. "But, I mean, sometimes I wonder if I blew my one chance, you know? Like maybe I was just being too practical and not letting go and letting God, or whatever the slogan is."

I nod to Eliza. "Your turn."

"My turn for what?"

"Were you ever close to getting married?"

"Oh," she waves a hand. "I've been proposed to about six times."

I start laughing and Ashten grins. "What?" I say. "From who?"

"Well, four of the times were from this guy in St. Louis who was in basically every single class I had until I went to college. He's pretty much been proposing since I was a sophomore in high school." She shakes her head. "He's ridiculous. And totally not my type."

"And the other two times?" Ashten asks.

"One was from a patient's husband, but that was more of a joke than anything. Bless their hearts. Their poor baby was not a happy camper to be outside the womb. I mean, most babies have a rough time, but I've never seen a kid who was as mad as this little guy. Basically, the dad asked if I would ever consider some sort of sister wives agreement, move in and be their baby's nanny."

"Ew," Ashten says, wrinkling her nose.

"Right? And then there was this guy in my nursing classes who thought we were going to be these missionary nurses, traveling to the remote jungles of the world, helping people there and telling them about Jesus. I was kind of like, yeah, but people need to hear about Jesus in our own backyard too, you know? I mean, it would be different if every patient I met was a Christian, but I promise you, they are not."

I smile at Eliza. She's not what I would call classically beautiful, but she's just so cute and straightforward, I can see why people like her so much.

"Anyway," she says, sipping from her Sprite. "That's my story and I'm sticking to it."

"And so here we are," Ashten says.

"Here we are," Eliza nods.

I pick up my Dr. Pepper and hold it up. "To new friendships," I say.

The girls follow suit and clink their glasses against mine. "To friendships."

"And to enjoying this stage of life to the fullest," Eliza nods.

I clink her glass and nod. "Yes," I say, sipping my drink and feeling my heart echo her thought in a prayer.

Please Lord. Help me enjoy this stage. And most of all, God, please help it just be a stage.

CHAPTER *Seven*

I sit down Friday morning to eat my breakfast while I check my email. The rest of the week passed in a blur of adverbs and I swear if I see another *ly*-word, I'm going to hit something.

I'd sent Joe a fairly scathing email last night just out of frustration. I do not understand how this novel passed the acquisitions team.

There's a reply from Joe sitting there this morning, but there's also an email from First Community right below it and I frown. How did they get my email address?

Welcome to First Community! it reads in the subject line. I click the message and it's a news filled email with all the latest happenings at the church. At the bottom of it, there's an announcement about the different Bible studies coming up this week.

I copy the link, send it to my phone and then text it to both Ashten and Eliza. Maybe they'll be interested in going to one with me. Goodness only knows I could use a good Bible study right now. Lately, I feel like all I do is complain.

A few years ago at the church I went to in New York, I remember a girl telling me that it wasn't respectful to question

God's plan for my life and if that meant that I was going to be single forever, well then I just needed to take one for the team, shut my mouth and throw out my laundry list of complaints when it came to that future for me.

Granted, the girl telling me this was two years older than me, had already been married for eight years and had four kids. She didn't really have a lot of experience when it came to singleness. I'd called my mom in tears over the conversation and Mom, bless her heart, told me over a screaming toddler that if God was big enough to create this whole world and to create me with this desire, then He could definitely handle some complaining from me. "If His hands are big enough to hold this whole world, then He doesn't have small shoulders, honey," Mom had told me. "He can handle your frustration, I guarantee."

I'd spent a little bit of time in the Psalms after that and noticed how often David complained. Which honestly made me feel a little better. I mean, he was supposed to be the man after God's own heart, right? If he could complain and not be smited for it, so could I.

I click Joe's email and it's sympathetic. I know he can't do anything about it, but he makes a good sounding board.

I finish my cup of coffee. Time to get to work.

By noon, I am banging my head on the desk.

My phone buzzes right then and I answer it without looking at the Caller ID. "Hello?"

"Hi honey, how are you?"

It's Gram. I rub my forehead. "Gram. I wish adverbs had never been invented."

"So how would you say that I walk to the car, then?"

"Slow and steady."

"Like the tortoise from that fable?"

"Sure."

"Mm. I'll take it. Listen, honey, I was calling about dinner tonight."

Gram usually calls on Thursdays to see what I want to have, so I was a little bit surprised not to hear from her yesterday.

"I was wondering if you could be at my house at six," she says.

"Sure, I can do that," I say. I usually get there a little bit earlier because she's always dying to eat by five, but later will work out fine. Though, Gram's an amazing cook and I was hoping that I would be done working early enough to go over and help her make dinner. And by "help", I mean that I want to watch her do it so I can maybe learn a couple of things. Like maybe how she makes her dumplings or biscuits.

You know how people have two left feet when they are terrible dancers? Yeah, I have two left hands when it comes to cooking. Particularly baking. I can brown ground beef and put ingredients into a pot for soup and whatever but I can't make anything bread-like for the life of me. Inevitably, the biscuits spread across the whole pan or are just floury blobs of burned grossness and I've never made a loaf of bread, even something supposedly easy like cornbread or muffins, that couldn't have doubled as a weight to prop open doors in the hot, humid summers.

Gram is still talking. "Lovely. Thank you, dear. Well, I will see you tonight!"

"Wait, Gram?"

"Yes, honey?"

I rub my cheek. She sounds like she's in a hurry. "Never mind. I'll see you tonight."

"Yes, you will. Don't forget, six o'clock. Not before."

"Six o'clock," I nod. "See you then, Gram."

"Bye now."

She hangs up and I click the red button on my phone and look at the screen on my computer. Just a few more hours. And really, I'm making good progress considering how many corrections I've had to do.

Monday is the quarterly staff meeting where they assign the next quarter's work docket to all the editors. Originally, I was supposed to go to New York for the meeting but then they decided that was silly and they could just conference call me and the other six or so editors who work outside the city. It works better for me anyway. The more often I travel, the more I hate it.

At five o'clock, I stop working and go take a shower, attempting to rinse the adverbs out of my hair along with the shampoo. I turn the water off, dry off and wrap the towel around my head. I pull on a pair of workout shorts and a tank top just to wear while I'm fixing my hair and getting my makeup on, because I have this weird thing about putting on jeans fresh out of the shower.

They just don't feel right.

It takes me ten minutes to work a comb through my wet hair and get some product in it. My hair is officially way too long. It's way past halfway down my back, which was always the longest I swore I would let it get. I am going to need to do something about this. I stare at it in the mirror. It's just weird. It's not blonde, it's not brown, it's not red. It's like some weird mix of all of the colors. And it's not totally wavy and it's not totally straight but some combination of both with a few sections that are more spiral curls than anything else.

I think about Eliza's straight, silky, shiny hair and sigh.

I rub in a volumizing serum and fluff my hair up as much as I can. Ninety percent of the time, I just let it air dry and go with whatever it looks like that day. If I want to look nice, I'll take the time to blow dry it. But not tonight. It's just Gram. She's seen me looking far worse. When I was a kid, every single time we came to visit Gram and Grandpa I would get sick. Usually with something awful like a stomach bug and one time I got pneumonia. It became something of a joke in the family.

I remember we would come for Thanksgiving or Christmas or in the summer for reunions and all my cousins would be playing outside or building snow forts or going to cool kid places like Planet Fun, and I would just get to lay on a blanket-covered couch the whole day with a throw-up bucket next to me. I was crying about having to stay home from the play place one time when I was about nine and Gram walked in, set a bowl of her homemade chicken soup that could cure basically anything from bronchitis to hangnails on the coffee table in front of me and just shook her head.

"All right, Katie-Kins, that is enough of that," she'd said. "If you're going to be sick every time you come, well then we are just going to have to create some of our own style of fun. Sound good?"

Then she popped *Anne of Green Gables* in the DVD player and I met Gilbert for the first time.

Gram and I have always had this special connection ever since. And there might have been a day or two when we visited where I would exaggerate my allergies or come up with a queasy stomach, just so that I could snuggle down on the sofa with one of Gram's hand-crocheted afghans, a bowl of chicken soup, Gram's shoulder to lay on and Gilbert on the screen.

I get to Gram's house at exactly six o'clock and knock on the door, holding the key to her house in my hand. I just can't do it. It's too weird to walk into someone's house unannounced.

"Good night, Katie, how many times do I have to tell you to use the key I gave you?" Gram asks, opening the door.

I smile. "Hey Gram."

"I'm getting too old to keep answering the door all night long."

"Well, thankfully, you only have to answer it for me," I say, closing and locking the door behind us.

We walk into the living room and there's a man sitting on Gram's couch. I jump.

"Hi," he says.

"Oh my gosh," I say. "You scared me to death!"

"Sorry about that."

"Katie, this is Jake. Jake, this is my granddaughter, Katie."

"Nice to meet you," Jake says, standing and nodding to me.

Uh-oh.

I instantly know what this is. Apparently, I should not have been so honest with Gram about my frustration in still being single.

Gram is standing there, grinning at us both and I realize that the dining room table that we never sit at is set with silverware and plates. There's a basket with a towel covered lump in the middle of the table. Likely her homemade rolls.

A set up is worth her homemade rolls.

Besides, Jake, so far, seems fairly nice. He's nice looking, anyway. Taller. Dark hair. Brown eyes. He's wearing jeans, a button down shirt and cowboy boots, so maybe he's a cowboy and we can fall in love and get married on a cattle ranch or something like what happened in a book series I edited one time.

I've always liked barn weddings.

Jake looks familiar to me. "Have we met before?" I ask and then instantly close my eyes. Here I am saying the exact same line twice in one week.

I am losing it. Thirty-one is causing me to reach new levels in pathetic. I mean, my grandmother is setting me up on a blind date and I'm not even mad about it. More just curious. And halfway thankful, because goodness knows I haven't met anyone in the last few months I've lived here.

Jake grins. "I heard you were at the wedding last weekend."

Apparently, so was most of the town.

Gram nods triumphantly. "She was there!"

"I was in the wedding. Kevin is one of my best friends. We went to college together," he says. I hear a buzz and Jake digs in his pocket, retrieving a phone. "Sorry about that. Just a minute," he mutters, clicking around on the screen.

Ah-ha. And it clicks for me. This is the groomsman who was on his phone the whole evening.

Gram doesn't seem to notice the technology interrupting us. "Well," she says, clapping her hands together. "Let's just sit down and eat then, shall we? I am starving. This is way beyond my preferred eating time for dinner."

"Gram, if we were eating at your preferred dinner time, it would already be time to eat again," I say, grinning at my grandmother.

She rewards my not-so-subtle dig at her habits with an eye roll. "Four-thirty is a perfectly acceptable time to eat dinner. The cafeteria even starts serving dinner then."

I shake my head. "Maybe the older you get, the more your appetite moves toward a different time zone."

"It's a heavenly time zone, dear."

I lift up a corner of the towel in the basket and Gram's homemade sweet dinner rolls are in there, just like I hoped.

Gram grins at me. "You're so predictable."

"Your rolls are amazing."

I don't sit because I know that we are just going to be grabbing our plates and moving to the kitchen to serve, so Gram and I just stand there by the table, waiting for Jake, who is still clicking around on his phone.

I have decided that the biggest thing I hate about my generation is the dumb cell phone attached to all of our hands. While I can see the convenience of having a flashlight that you can find by calling it, it honestly makes me nuts that no one can move three feet without moving their cell phone right along with them.

I look across the table at Gram and she smiles at me. *He's cute, huh?* she mouths.

Well, I've mostly seen the top of his head, so I guess I don't know for certain. Though, he's held onto his hair. That's a plus.

He makes a noise in the back of his throat and shoves his phone back into his pocket. "So sorry about that," he says, walking over to join us at the table. "It smells amazing in here, Mrs. Laughlin."

"Well, thank you very much. Now, grab your plates and follow me into the kitchen."

We follow Gram and she's outdone herself with chicken fried steak, mashed potatoes and gravy and green bean casserole. It's like the Thanksgiving of artery-clogging foods. I'm sort of wishing I hadn't spent the entire day plugging away at Sue's book and had instead stopped working a little bit earlier and worked out.

But I ladle an extra-large helping of potatoes and gravy on my plate and inwardly shrug. There's always tomorrow.

I can never remember if Shirley Temple or Scarlett O'Hara said that.

Or maybe it was that girl with the obnoxiously high voice on one of those animated Santa Claus movies?

"Gram, this looks amazing," I tell her, sitting down across from her at the table.

"It's a feast, ma'am," Jake nods from the head of the table.

"Thank you both. Why don't we go ahead and pray?" Gram folds her hands in her lap and I'm thankful that she didn't try to be extra-Mrs.-Bennet –like and make us hold hands for the prayer. She prays a short, quick prayer and then picks up her fork.

"So, Jake, how long have you lived in Carrington Springs?" Gram asks.

"Oh, about three years, ma'am," he says. I hear another buzz and out comes the phone again. "So sorry, so sorry," he mumbles again, clicking around.

I mean, seriously.

I hack off a bite of chicken fried steak and thoroughly douse it in gravy before putting it in my mouth. Maybe I shouldn't be so quick to judge. Maybe he uses his cell phone for work or something and he's on call tonight. Maybe he's the one in charge of donor hearts for the hospital or something and he has to be within reach at all times.

Gram and I eat our dinner in relative quiet because nothing kills normal small talk like a stranger who is physically present, but lost in a world of two-dimensional problems and people.

He shoves his phone back in his pocket with a click. "So sorry," he says again, picking up his fork and knife. "Yes, ma'am, I've been here three years," he repeats.

"What do you do?" Gram asks.

I'm waiting for the Must Be Able To Be Reached At All Times job. Heart surgeon. Obstetrician. Goodness, even a political advisor to someone running for governor would count at this point.

"I'm kind of in between careers right now. I'm back in school and I deliver papers as well."

Gram, bless her heart, doesn't change her expression. "What are you studying in school, Jake?"

"I'm going to be an electrician."

Gram nods. "A fine job. We need some good and honest electricians in this town. Goodness only knows what I would do if I lived by myself. My husband wasn't the best at home improvement projects. I remember we had one electrician come out to fix our garbage disposal. He almost took us for every cent we were worth and he didn't even fix it."

"I'm sorry to hear that," Jake says. "And you have a roommate?"

"Oh no. I meant if I lived off the retirement center property. They come and take care of everything now. They even change my light bulbs for me."

"Wow," Jake says.

"It's really a wonderful place to live," Gram says. "Especially before my dear granddaughter arrived and I was living in this town by myself. Next time a light bulb goes out, I'm just going to call Katie."

I smirk. "So I can call the front desk?"

"Watch it, honey. I did make your favorite rolls."

"Sorry Gram. I will change your light bulbs any time you need them changed. Day or night."

"That's better."

Buzz.

"So sorry, so sorry," Jake mutters again, pulling back out the phone.

I shake my head to myself and keep eating the delicious dinner. Even Gram is frowning at Jake now.

Well, whatever he's doing is obviously not work-related nor is it likely saving lives.

We finish eating, Gram pulls out a pecan pie for dessert and I set my fork down after I inhale a slice, totally and completely stuffed to the absolute top of my head. Even the thought of more food is making me a little bit sick.

"Gram," I say, hefting out a breath. "You outdid yourself tonight. That was a feast."

"It was really good, ma'am. Thank you."

"You are both welcome."

Buzz. Buzz.

Neither Gram nor I try to contain our sighs this time.

"Honey, is there some sort of an emergency going on tonight?" Gram asks Jake as he pulls out his cell phone for the ninetieth time that night. I mean, it would have been a lot easier on his jeans' pocket if he'd just left it on the table.

Jake looks up from his phone. "I'm sorry?"

"Your phone, son. You have barely looked at me or my beautiful granddaughter all night."

Well, if we had any doubt that this was basically a blind date, now we know. I'm too frustrated with the cell phone to even blush.

"Oh no, ma'am. I'm sorry." He puts it back in his pocket. Ten seconds later, it buzzes again.

We both just look at him.

"Thanks for a wonderful meal," Jake says, standing. "I think I should probably be going though."

"You need to lock that phone in your trunk so you can't get to it while you're driving," Gram says, still in lecture mode.

"Uh, that's a good idea, ma'am. I might have to do that."

"No, you should do that. I've seen some very ugly pictures of car wrecks from when the driver was texting."

"Yes ma'am. Nice to meet you, Katie."

He lets himself out.

Gram and I just sit there at the table and Gram sighs. "Well, that did not go how I had planned it out in my head. Good graciousness, I swear that boy never stopped looking at that cell phone of his." She shakes her head. "Makes me nervous about him driving. Frieda told me just the other day about a terrible accident between here and St. Louis that they determined was caused by someone driving and looking at their phone. Caused a four car pileup and two people died, including a child." She rubs her cheek. "News like that just makes me long for heaven even more."

I nod. "I'm with you, Gram."

"You don't look at your phone while you're driving, do you?"

"No."

"Good." She shakes her head at the door. "Well, so much for dinner. Such a shame. Poor kid was nice looking. And polite."

"Everyone has their flaws, I guess."

"Well, speak for yourself," Gram grins, winking at me.

"Sorry. Most everyone has their faults."

"That's better." She stands and starts stacking plates. "Well, we will just scratch him off the list and move on to the next one."

"Oh Gram, you didn't really make a list, did you?" I can't decide if I'm more embarrassed or curious about who is on this list. And how does my grandmother know all these single men and I have hardly met any?

"Frieda's grandson is single," Gram says. "I believe he's the next one up."

I think about Gram's feisty friend and try to imagine a man with those genetics.

He could be…interesting.

Then again, maybe he would take after his grandfather. Though he seemed fairly spunky, too.

"Well, what's he like?" I ask, helping Gram carry the plates and utensils into the kitchen. I grab the nearly empty bread basket too. Jake could eat and text with the best of them.

"I don't know, I've never met him."

"Does he live here?"

Gram shrugs. "I don't know. Frieda just called me up after the wedding and said that you and her grandson would be perfect together."

"I don't know how I feel about that."

Gram laughs. "No one ever knows how they feel when they are around Frieda," she tells me.

Yes, I could see how this would be the case.

CHAPTER *Eight*

I am parked in front of First Community on Saturday night, gripping the steering wheel because I know that this is a terrible idea.

Who am I? I don't go to Bible studies to meet men. Isn't that bad? Isn't it taking the priority off the Bible and putting it on other people? Would the Apostle Paul be hitting me over the head with his Biblical scrolls right now?

I stare at the front of the church and squeeze my eyes tight. *Lord, just...I don't know, actually. Just keep me from doing something I shouldn't.*

Gram told me last Friday night as I was helping her clean the kitchen that I needed to expand my "circle of influence."

"Katie," she'd said. "When I met your grandfather, I was nineteen and marrying men were plenty. That's not the case anymore, honey. You have to make yourself available."

"What are you asking me to do, Gram?"

"Nothing improper, trust me. But just think about Ruth in the Bible. She didn't just sit in her little shack and wait for Boaz to come find her, did she?"

"Um, well—"

"No," Gram had interrupted. "She didn't! She took the corn by the ears and went out there and found herself a man."

I was fairly certain that Ruth was actually more intending to find food to keep her and her mother-in-law alive rather than finding a husband, but I hadn't commented on it. Or on the weird "corn by the ears" thing, whatever that meant.

I've put myself out there before. A lot of times. And usually I end up just feeling out of place or weird. And now, I'm usually one of the oldest in these "single Bible studies" like First Community had advertised on their email newsletter.

I check my makeup in the mirror, grab my Bible and my purse and step out of the car, taking a deep breath.

"Hey! Katie, over here!"

It's Eliza and she's waiting with Ashten just to the left of the front doors. I walk across the parking lot and join them.

"Hey," I say, trying not to appear as nervous as I am. It's not like I'm going by myself, right?

"You look terrified," Eliza says.

I huff out a breath and nervously tuck a strand of hair behind my ear. "Thanks."

"No, I mean, seriously," Eliza says. "Have you never been to a Bible study before?"

"I just hate going to new things," I say.

Ashten nods. "It's not my favorite either, Katie."

"Come on, guys! It will be fun! I love meeting new people!" Eliza says, putting her arms around us both and guiding us into the church.

There are about twenty or thirty people milling around the foyer, talking, laughing and most are holding coffee cups. To my surprise, it doesn't look like I'm the oldest one here, either.

There are a lot of people who look like they are probably in their thirties.

Though, who knows these days. The whole beard craze has totally changed the ability to know someone's true age. To be honest, I can't stand it. I think beards are gross. Even the thought of hair spontaneously growing out of your cheeks is just weird.

"Hi there."

A blond couple who are either married or siblings approach the three of us and I can see the thoughts going through all of our heads. Married or related? Couples like these always tend to weird me out. If they are married, do they not see the resemblance? And if they aren't, should siblings really stand that close?

"Hi," Ashten finally says.

"Hey," I say.

Eliza is still in puppy-cock mode.

"We just noticed some new faces and wanted to introduce ourselves," the man says. "I'm Ben and this is Melissa and we're really glad you joined us today!"

"What are your names?" Melissa asks.

"I'm Katie, this is Ashten and Eliza," I say, since Ashten immediately looks at me and Eliza still has her head tipped.

"Well, it's really nice to have you here. Please grab a cup of coffee. We're going to actually be meeting in the youth room in a few minutes."

They walk away. Still no answer to our mystery.

"They have to be related," Eliza declares.

"Shh," Ashten shushes her. "You need to keep your voice down. We don't know that they are related."

"Totally related. They have the same nose!"

"Everyone's nose looks similar to someone else's," Ashten says.

"Let's get some coffee," I say and lead the other two in the general direction the Ben person had nodded when he was talking about the coffee.

There's a Keurig machine sitting on a high counter with a bunch of boxes of the little plastic cups next to it and a huge assortment of mugs on the other side of the machine.

Ah, the robotic barista. I've been thinking about getting one of these so I wasn't constantly throwing out coffee that had been sitting on the burner for four hours while I was working.

Eliza immediately pulls a cup out of the chai tea latte box and puts it in the machine, clicking the button and filling a large purple mug with the steaming, golden liquid. Ashten carefully sorts through the boxes, reading the descriptions on the sides and slightly shaking her head when I guess it doesn't sound good to her. She ends up going for a hazelnut coffee and adding a healthy spoonful of sugar and a good quarter cup of cream to it.

"Not a coffee fan?" Eliza asks her. "You should have gone with the chai latte. This is amazing."

"I just prefer water, mostly," Ashten says. "Or orange juice. My grandma makes this spiced tea that we sell at the restaurant and I really like that too."

"Hot or iced?" I ask her.

"Hot. It's the only hot drink I can really stand. I'm just not a hot drink person." She sips her coffee and makes a face. "I wish I was. But I'm just not."

"You didn't have to get anything," Eliza tells her.

"I know but sometimes I try things just to see if I've changed at all. And I haven't."

"So what do you drink if it's snowing outside?" I ask her.

"Yeah? Like first thing in the morning when you wake up and it's snowing and there's Christmas music on and the tree is all lit up?" Eliza says.

Ashten shrugs. "Orange juice."

Eliza an I exchange a look and we both just shake our heads.

"New project," Eliza says.

I grin. I pop the darkest decaf roast I can find into the Keurig and watch the dark coffee spit out. The darker, the better when it comes to my coffee. I just can't do caffeine at night anymore.

A sure sign of old age, I think.

"All right, everyone, let's go ahead and go on into the room," the blond man yells from the doorway of what I guess is the youth room.

Everyone who is busy talking starts moving in that direction. My coffee finishes, I add a little sugar and cream and follow Eliza and Ashten into the room.

The room looks like what I imagine ninety percent of youth rooms in churches across America look like. There are four long, beat up and mismatched couches, a bunch of bean bag chairs thrown around on the floor and about fifteen folding chairs that are all different colors. A rickety metal podium is in front of everything and there's a folded up ping pong table against the back wall.

It's like a couple of garage sales chewed up their leftovers and spit them out into this room.

But somehow it works. And as people pile onto the couches and flounce onto the bean bag chairs and sit nicely on the folding chairs, I can see why this space is conducive to youth.

But it's not necessarily conducive to a bunch of older-ish single people.

"Come on in, come on in." The blond man is standing by the podium and I've decided he's the leader of the group. "All right, how was everyone's week?" He nods to a dark-haired, semi-balding man on a red bean bag on the floor. "Matt, let's start with you."

Everyone gets a turn to say how their week went. Most people shared work stories and honestly, a lot of stuff involving dogs and cats and a bunch of stuff no one really cares about. One girl starts crying as she talks about a work problem she's having and another guy updates everyone on how he's now been out of a job for seven months.

"But you know, I just keep praying. I know God has a plan for this and maybe it was just so I could reconnect with my parents again," he says.

I want to ask how his parents are doing with him back in the house, but I don't say anything.

On and on it goes. Work problems, cat/dog problems, apartment or rental house problems.

I'm starting to tune it out.

It gets quiet and I start a little bit when everyone is just looking at me. "Oh sorry, I'm Katie," I say, nervously fidgeting with my empty coffee cup. "I'm new here tonight."

"How was your week, Katie? Any way we can be praying for you?"

I think through my life and there's nothing I really feel like telling a group of total strangers. "I had a good week, thank you." I look at Eliza and she nods.

"I'm Eliza and I'm with Katie, actually. I had a great week."

Ashten stops biting her bottom lip long enough to say the same thing. Based on their responses, I think we are all having the same thought.

By the time the blond man gets all the way around the group and everyone has a chance to complain, I mean share how their week went, it's been almost forty-five minutes. The man nods to the last teary-eyed girl and then looks at the podium. "All right, so let's be sure to be in prayer for each other this week. Couple of announcements, we've got that Starbucks social thing coming up and I believe that Rick's parents are hosting a barbecue this next weekend for us. Is that right, Rick?"

The guy who is jobless and living with his parents nods. "Yeah, they said for everyone to bring a side to share."

"Great. So bring a side. Thanks for coming guys. Let's close in prayer."

He prays a short prayer and everyone starts chattering amongst themselves. I look at Eliza and Ashten.

"Dessert?" Eliza asks and we are out of the room and agreeing to meet at Chili's a few minutes later.

Eliza is the first one there and the waitress is already leading her back to a table when Ashten and I walk in. We sit down, she hands us the menus, we decide on something to eat and then we all simultaneously sigh.

"Seriously," Eliza nods.

"I'm not sure that should really be called a Bible study," Ashten says softly.

"It definitely shouldn't," I shake my head. "We didn't study anything. Not one thing. It was like everyone just came to sit around and complain about their lives."

Eliza nods. "Other than the three of us, I don't think another person said they'd had a good week. I mean, I am a fairly positive person, but I could feel all that positivity leaching out of me in there." She shakes her head. "Sorry, Katie. I know you were wanting to join a Bible study, but I don't think I can go back there."

"Me either," Ashten says.

I nod. "I'm not going either. The only people who talked to us were the blond twins. Did we ever find out if they were married or related?"

Eliza shakes her head. "Seriously. They have the same nose. They are totally siblings. So ew."

I grin.

"I feel like we should go around the table and say things that are good God has given us right now," Ashten says.

The waitress shows up right then for our orders and we all hand over our menus and tell her what we'd like to eat. She leaves and Eliza slaps her hands on the table.

"I'll start," she declares. "There are so many good things in my life right now! I took care of four healthy babies who were all born yesterday and all of them were getting discharged today. I learned that I cannot cook gumbo and I will never try again. I am about to have molten chocolate cake for dessert with two people who are quickly becoming some of my favorite people on earth and I have officially decided that I am never getting a pet."

Ashten grins. "That was a good list, Eliza."

"Your turn."

Ashten nods. "Okay. So I am going to echo Eliza and say that I am very thankful for the two of you. I had a great week with my class and two of my lowest kids scored fantastically on the reading quiz I gave them yesterday after our Dr. Seuss unit. And I got to make green eggs and ham this week which was just fun."

"How did they taste?" I ask.

"Disgusting, but that's beside the point," Ashten grins.

I laugh. "Okay, my turn. I'm thankful for my Gram and her excellent cooking. I'm thankful that I don't live in New York anymore and for the fall leaves." The waitress sets our desserts in front of us and I inhale right above my skillet cookie. "And I'm very thankful for this."

"And us," Eliza adds.

"Of course you guys."

"Can I pray real quick?" Ashten asks and then just starts without really waiting for a response. "Jesus, thank You for these friends and for our food. Please help us to honor You with our words. Amen."

"Amen," Eliza and I echo.

Eliza's molten chocolate cake would probably look amazing if I liked desserts that were squishy in the middle. I have this huge fear of raw eggs, thanks to my mother, so I can't stand runny baked goods. I always get freaked out by listeria or salmonella or whatever it is that under cooked eggs can cause.

Ashten ordered nachos and I just shake my head at her.

"What?" she asks.

"Nachos? It's a dessert night," I say, pointing to mine and Eliza's desserts.

"It sounded good with my Coke."

"We really need to help you understand coffee," Eliza says, sipping her decaf.

"It's not a matter of understanding," Ashten says. "I just like ice in my drinks. Or it to be a citrusy juice."

"Have you tried iced coffee?" I ask. "I mean, Frappucinos were my gateway drug, so maybe it would be the same for you."

She shrugs. "I can buy a gallon of orange juice that I am just as happy with for the same amount of a small drink at Starbucks. I figure I might as well save the money and still be as happy. Except happier, I guess, because I have a few more dollars in my pocket."

Eliza lifts her mug to Ashten. "More power to you, my friend. I wish I had the same level of carelessness about it as you do. But sadly, the addiction is pretty much in full swing."

Ashten grins. "Don't worry, I think I'm in the minority. At least you have company."

I half listen to their conversation while I stir one of those little plastic cup creamers into my coffee and watch the ice cream melt on my skillet cookie.

Here's the thing: I feel like all we heard tonight was a list of complaints. And not even good complaints, most of them were so shallow it just makes me cringe.

But then I think about my laundry list of complaints for Jesus and I just start to get a little fidgety in the booth. What if I am just like them? What if my complaints are just as shallow, just as hard to listen to as the people we were with tonight? What if Jesus sits up in heaven and cringes just as much as I was down here tonight?

"I think we lost Katie," Eliza says, elbowing me. "Earth to Katie! How you doing over there?"

"Do you ever wonder what Jesus thinks of you?" I ask.

Both of them give me a blank stare. "Um, what exactly do you mean?" Ashten says finally.

I take a deep breath and try to put my thoughts into words. "Like, we're all sitting here talking about how much complaining happened at the 'Bible study' tonight," I say, using my fingers as quotations around the words. "But, I mean, if I'm being totally honest, I'd say a good ninety percent of my prayers sound just like those complaints we heard tonight, you know? It just makes me wonder if Jesus is up there cringing and shaking His head like we are doing down here."

Eliza and Ashten are quiet for a few minutes. Eliza sips her coffee, Ashten crunches her nachos.

"I mean, I would probably say no," Ashten says finally.

"Why not?" I ask.

"Well, I mean, you have to look at it differently. First off, I'm not upset with the people for complaining. What bothered me is that they called tonight a Bible study when we didn't open our Bibles once."

"Yep. With you there," Eliza nods.

"But, we also aren't Jesus. You know? I mean, He loves us. He cares for us. And I know we don't have kids, but I have a bunch of friends who do and they've told me a few times that it has totally changed the way they view their relationship with God. Because if He calls Himself our Father, then He wants to know everything that is going on with us. Just like my friends like to hear what's going on with their kids, even if it's just little stuff. You know?" she says again.

Eliza sighs. "Yeah, but I mean, honestly, how much do your friends like listening to their kids complain about things?"

"Right," I say. "That's what I'm thinking too. Because I've met people and known people who complain all day long and it gets really old really fast."

Ashten shrugs. "I don't know. I feel like Jesus can handle our complaints."

"But it feels like constantly complaining is sort of being ungrateful for what we've been given," I say.

"And I don't know why everyone there was complaining anyway," Eliza says, shaking her head. "I mean, this is the best we are ever going to feel, the best health we are ever going to be in, the youngest we are ever going to be again. We should be climbing mountains and playing Frisbee and doing accomplishments like...I don't know...building bridges or something," she says, waving her hand that isn't holding her coffee in the air.

Ashten grins. "I'll get right to work on that bridge for you."

"It was just an illustration, smarty pants."

"Yeah, based on my test scores in geometry, I'm not sure that anyone wants to be walking or driving across a bridge that had anything to do with me," I say, shaking my head.

"Exactly. Though I could totally plant some ivy or something so it grew up around the bridge," Ashten says.

"Oh!" I am nodding. "That would be gorgeous!"

"Look, guys, forget the bridge," Eliza says, rolling her eyes and setting down her coffee. "My point is that we are young, we are beautiful and we are in the prime of our lives." She ticks the points off on her fingers. "So, why are we sitting around on bean bag chairs complaining about everything and owning cats?"

"I don't actually own a cat," says Ashten.

"Neither do I," I say. "I think I'm allergic to them."

"I'm a dog person," Ashten says.

"I really don't care for animals, period," I say. "I don't even like going to the zoo, to be honest. I had some neighbors in New York who owned parrots and the things screamed bloody murder all day. But, if you called the apartment supervisor, they were quiet as church mice."

"Ew. Mice." Ashten shivers.

"So ever since then, I have hated birds, too."

"I never liked them, either," Ashten says. "I was always kind of voting for the Coyote to get the Roadrunner."

Eliza closes her eyes and picks up her coffee. "I give up."

CHAPTER *Nine*

Monday morning, I am up, dressed and backing out of my driveway at eight o'clock. I am going to finish Sue's book today, I am going to eat a pumpkin scone while I'm doing it and I am going to need unlimited refills of coffee to get it done.

And a fireplace.

So, Panera it is. The Panera by my house is definitely more of a lunch destination than a breakfast one, so it's basically empty when I get there. I find the best table that is close to both the fireplace and the outlet and I plop my computer and all my notes down before heading to the line.

I order my scone and my coffee and try not to be obvious as I walk back to my table, surreptitiously glancing around.

I mean, I didn't think he would be here.

I would have done my makeup and made sure my hair looked a little less like a mop of weird curls and waves even if I hadn't met the cute Luke Brantley last time I was here.

I shake my head and turn on my laptop, trying to focus on the task at hand. Time to buckle on my editor helmet and get to work. I'm so over this book. And I've already been slotted for three more novels for the next three months.

I sent Joe an email asking about when I was supposed to enjoy my holidays and he told me that I would be enjoying the money, if not the time off.

126

Bah humbug.

I'm sixty pages into my work load for the day and on my fifth refill by the time noon comes around. I've already emailed Joe three times with samples of what I'm editing and he's sent me back those teary-eyed emojis and a couple of violins. I can never tell whether the emojis are laughing or crying.

Maybe both.

I'm starting to get a little hungry and the place is filling up with people coming in for a soup fix since it's fall and wonderfully colorful and crisp outside. There's hardly an empty table in the restaurant now and I'm thankful I came when I did and got the good one.

Time for a lunch break.

I save my work and stand in line, debating what I want, but knowing that I'll get the same thing I always get, even if something else sounds good. I always think I want to try something new at my favorite restaurants until I'm ordering and then I realize what I'm saying and change it as fast as I can. I actually did order something new one time. It was awful and ever since then, I've been jaded toward new things.

I order my broccoli cheese soup in a bread bowl, take my pager to my table and work a little more while I'm waiting for them to bring it over.

"Couldn't resist the fireplace, I see."

I look up and it's Luke Brantley, the oldies singer with the country music name, sitting down at a table across the aisle from me.

I smile. "It's the best seat in the house."

"Oh, I know this. I know it well. Except for days like today." He nods to the sunny day outside. "I'm not a fan of fireplaces when the sun is out."

"Why not?"

"I don't know. They make me feel weird. It's sort of like making s'mores when you aren't camping. It just shouldn't be done."

"What about people who have backyard fire pits?" I ask.

"Don't even get me started on backyard fire pits," he says, holding up a hand and I grin.

"Broccoli cheese in a bread bowl and a side salad," the waitress says, setting the tray down next to my computer. "Can I get you anything else?"

"No thanks."

"Have a good lunch."

"Thanks."

Luke is tsking at his table. "Got the soup again, huh? Why order it in a bread bowl if you aren't going to eat the bowl?"

"I eat the inside of it. Sometimes I eat the outside." I shrug. "I don't know, there's just something fun about ordering soup in a bread bowl."

"Sort of like those little sorbet things that come inside the fruits?"

I frown. "Not sure I know what you're talking about."

"You know? The ones where they half a lemon and pull out the insides and fill it with sorbet? Or when people serve fruit salad inside a watermelon rind?"

I nod. "I have seen that before."

"I was at a wedding one time where they served fruit salad to each person inside an orange rind."

I nod. "Huh."

"Yeah. It was weird. And not very much fruit either."

I grin.

The waitress comes and sets his sandwich and salad in front of him and he nods to her. "Thanks."

"Sure thing. Hey, do I know you from somewhere?" she asks, taking his pager.

It would seem that Luke Brantley gets this question a lot. Though, if you get into the right wedding crowds in a fairly small town, you could be seen by pretty much everyone.

He hands the waitress one of his cards and explains to her how he does weddings on the weekends and she starts nodding as soon as she sees his picture on the card.

"Oh yeah!" she says. "You sang at my cousin's wedding a few months ago. You look a lot different on your card and on the stage than you do in person."

He shrugs. "I get that a lot. It's the glasses." He adjusts the black frames a little bit.

The girl looks at him, lips pursed. "And the hair," she says. "And the lack of a tux."

"I try not to wear the tux while I'm eating," he says.

She laughs and pockets the card. "Well, I'll be calling you soon, I'm sure," she says. "My fiancé and I loved your singing. It's totally the style we want. Thanks for the card."

"Thank you," he nods.

She goes back to the kitchen.

"Do I really look that different?" he asks me.

Well, that's a good and awkward question. The answer is obviously yes, but I don't know how to say that without sounding weird.

There's about two minutes of awkward silence as I open and close my mouth like one of those creepy deep water fish as I am mentally trying to figure out how to say it as delicately as possible.

"I'll take that as a yes," he says.

I wish I was more like Eliza. She wouldn't have cared about being delicate. She would have just told him straight out that he looked like a totally different person than the picture on his card.

I watch him duck his head for a minute over his lunch. Is he praying? Maybe he's a Christian.

I have reached new levels of desperation when even the thought of a potentially nice, seemingly polite man who prays over his deli sandwich is causing the "Wedding March" to start playing in my head.

Is it just me? Am I the only one who is constantly cataloguing men I meet into Potential Soul Mate and No Way in Heck? I close my eyes for a second and rub my temples. It's a terrible habit. One that I need to figure out how to change. How do you change your thought processes that are so ingrained into your brain, you do things without even thinking?

I remember being at a youth conference with our church about fifteen or so years ago, and the speaker on the stage was talking about how important it was to have a list of qualities you wanted in a future spouse.

"You don't go to the store without a list, so why would you approach marriage any differently?" he'd shouted into the microphone.

I remember writing his words down feverishly as he talked because I thought that he was totally inspired.

Now, it just sounds ridiculous.

Marriage isn't even in the same ballpark as a shopping trip. Why compare the two? And The List, the one I've held on to for ages and honed and rewritten and cried over and prayed over and begged God for, is now buried in one of my boxes in the garage.

"So how long have you lived in Carrington Springs?" Luke Brantley asks, twisting slightly in his chair so he's facing me as he eats his sandwich.

I don't know why I can't disconnect his first and last name in my head.

"About nine weeks," I tell him.

"Okay, so a newcomer. Well, it's good to have you here."

"How long have you been here?" I ask.

He swallows a bite of his sandwich and takes a drink of the fizzing Coke beside him. "I was actually born and raised here, but I moved away for college. Just came back about two years ago."

I reach for my spoon, since it appears that we are now going to be continuing this conversation over lunch. "So, does your family still live here?"

He nods again. "It's just me and my mom. My father hasn't been in the picture since I was about four. But my grandparents live here too, so that's nice."

"Oh. I'm sorry," I say and immediately wish I hadn't asked. Now it is just weird because I'm sure he'll ask about my family next.

"What about you? Where does your family live?"

See?

I try to brush it off. "Oh, not anywhere close to here. My grandmother lives in town though, which was the biggest selling point for moving to Carrington Springs."

He looks at me thoughtfully. "It's a blessing to come from a strong family, Katie. Not something to be ashamed about."

Lovely. He's apparently one of those people who can see right through my forehead and into my thoughts.

Fabulous.

"Where did you move here from?" he asks, continuing the conversation as he picks up his sandwich.

"New York," I say.

"Like the city?" he asks.

"One and the same."

"Very cool," he says, nodding his head as he eats. Meanwhile, I still haven't even put my spoon into my soup. "I've been there twice and always wondered if it was as awful living there as it is visiting."

I grin. "You get used to it."

He shakes his head. "I don't think I could. Not when I've spent the majority of my life in little Carrington Springs. You can take the boy out of the country but you can't take the country out of the boy, like people have said before."

I shrug. "I don't know. My boss in New York was actually from a tiny town in Indiana. He said he couldn't wait to get to the big city."

"He wasn't a true country boy then."

"And you are?"

Luke Brantley shrugs. "I don't know. I like it here, I know that much. It's a big enough city that you don't see the same people everywhere you go, but it's a small enough town that you occasionally bump into people you wouldn't mind seeing again." He grins at me. "Like today."

I'm trying my best not to blush.

I don't feel like it is going well.

"What did you do in New York? Editing?"

We are again verging on a lot of information for someone who I really don't know that well. And honestly, anyone can duck their head down for a few seconds before eating. It doesn't mean he was praying. And if he was, it doesn't mean he was praying to God. We live in a weird world these days. He could just be one of those twisted predators who sucks women in with his messy-haired good looks and flannel-shirt country charm.

I use the silence to take a bite of my now lukewarm soup. Time to go on the offense and ask him some questions.

"So, when did you start singing?" I ask, trying to play it off like I'd forgotten or hadn't heard his earlier question.

I think he knows that I'm trying to avoid the answer, but he's gracious about it. "High school," he says. "I started singing in church after my voice finally changed. My mom wanted me to sing earlier than that, but have you ever heard a kid in the middle of puberty trying to sing Sinatra?" He shakes his head and grimaces while I grin.

"Can't say that I have."

"Well, it's not pretty, I'll leave it at that."

I bite my bottom lip and risk a personal-ish question. "So, what church do you go to?"

"Cross Point." He nods. "I've been going there since before it was Cross Point. Way back when, it was Oakwood Baptist and I guess the elders decided that was just an old school name. So when we built a new building, they gave us a new name."

"Cross Point." I feel like I've seen it when I've been driving around.

"Yep. Heard of us?"

"I think so," I say slowly. "I want to say I saw the name and thought it was a gym."

He laughs. "We get that a lot. I still think we should go back to Oakwood Baptist, but I think I'm in the minority. Are you looking for a church? You should check us out."

I actually have no idea if I'm looking for a church or not. I went back to First Community yesterday and sat with Ashten and Eliza. The sermon was good, the music was good.

It's just weird that the Bible study we tried was so not good when everything else about the church is just what I want.

I hate when that happens.

"I'm not sure," I say to Luke Brantley.

"Well, I'd love to talk to you more about my church and about what it means to have a relationship with Jesus," he says to me.

I realize he took my not being sure as not being sure about church in general and I shake my head. "Oh no, I mean, I already have a relationship with Jesus," I tell him. "I meant that I'm not sure about the church. I've gone to First Community twice now and I have a couple of friends who go there, too."

He nods. "Oh, okay. Well, that's good to hear. And if you guys ever want to join us, you know that you are more than welcome. I think I gave you my card, right? Feel free to text me anytime."

"Thanks," I say.

"You're welcome." He looks at his watch and wipes his mouth with his napkin. He finished his whole meal during our conversation and I ate two bites of soup. "Well, I hate to leave in the middle of our conversation, but I have a video conference in twenty minutes with a client."

"Okay," I say.

"Have a great afternoon, Katie. Don't forget to at least eat some of the bread bowl." He grins at me, packs up his bag and leaves with a one handed wave.

CHAPTER *Ten*

Tuesday night, I'm scrounging through my kitchen looking for something to eat. Gram had sent me home with chicken fried steak leftovers, but as wonderful and delicious as chicken fried steak is when it is freshly made, something really awful happens to it in the refrigerator.

Just tragic. Especially since she sent me home with a whole Tupperware full of it.

I've already eaten all of the mashed potatoes and I'm pretty sure her amazing rolls were gone even before I pulled back into my driveway Friday night.

Maybe I should eat a light dinner considering all that.

I find a cucumber and a bag of baby carrots that are expiring tomorrow, so I cut them both up and a pour a glass of iced tea. It sounds all good and healthy, but I also have a package of Oreos in the cabinet I'm pretty sure I'll be eating while I watch Netflix tonight, so I'm just delaying calories.

I sit down on the sofa and pick up the remote. Then I look over at my Bible sitting on the coffee table. Saturday night after the Bible study that wasn't a Bible study, Ashten and Eliza decided we should start our own study through the Bible. We were all supposed to do some research this week and put in our recommendation for what book we think would be the best to work through.

136

I haven't had the time to do it yet during the day. I forgot last night. Instead, I watched four episodes of *Friday Night Lights* before collapsing into bed.

Nothing like a TV show starring a bunch of teenagers who all look like they are in their mid-twenties to make you appreciate your quiet, fairly drama-free life.

I set the remote down and pick up my Bible.

I rub my fingers over the cover and bite my bottom lip. About five years ago, this book was almost constantly in my hand. I read it on my lunch breaks, I read it on subways, I read it in taxis. I downloaded sermons and listened to them while I was doing mundane things like cleaning the toilet and shaving my legs.

Now, things are...I don't know. Different.

Back then, I thought maybe if I just got closer to Jesus, He would bring the right guy into my life. I threw everything I had into that relationship and for awhile, it didn't really matter that someone else never came along.

Then, it was like the wedding bus hit my hometown. Six of my old friends got married in the same three months and two friends in New York who had sworn off men in favor of their careers found boyfriends.

And there I was. Alone in my apartment with my sermons.

It was disheartening, to say the least.

Things changed after that summer. I don't know why, but they just did and I've never been able to get back to that same place. I thought maybe moving here was my answer, but it doesn't seem like it is.

I open the Bible and you can tell the Psalms were some of my favorites. And Paul's letters. I flip through it, crunching carrot sticks. Maybe one of Paul's letters would be a good one?

I flip a little too far and end up in First John.

John talks a lot about brotherly love in this book. Maybe we should do this one instead?

I'll suggest it.

I grab a cucumber slice and the remote. Time for some football team drama before heading back to working on the book.

I answer the phone on Wednesday as I'm typing my final comments for Sue in an email.

I finished it. I finally finished the book. I'm exhausted and I will never use an adverb again as long as I live, but I finished it.

I don't even look at the name on the screen, I just answer the call. "Hello?"

"Hey Katie, it's Eliza."

"Hey, what's up?"

"Not much. Do you have dinner plans tonight?"

I stick the phone in between my shoulder and my cheek and keep typing. "Dinner?"

"Right. Do you already have plans?"

I pause long enough to look at the clock display at the top of my computer screen. Almost five-thirty.

Right on cue, my stomach starts to growl.

"Nope, no dinner plans," I tell her.

"Great! You're coming over here," she says. "I'm about to call Ashten, too. I made this new recipe I saw on the Pioneer Woman and it made enough for about forty-three people."

I grin. "I've heard that about her recipes."

"Seriously. You'd think I would have learned after I made her cinnamon rolls one time and ran out of pans to put them in. But those were the most amazing rolls I've ever eaten in my whole life."

Now I want cinnamon rolls. "You didn't happen to make the rolls for tonight, did you?" I ask.

"Nope. Made soup and some bread. Smells good, so we'll see how it tastes."

"Can I bring anything?"

"Just yourself. Come over anytime."

"Okay. I'm finishing up some work and then I'll head over."

"Great!" She says goodbye and hangs up the phone. I finish typing my email. I read back through it and attach the document I've been electronically marking up.

The days of editing have changed so much. It's so convenient to never have to print out a novel. Though, I still do occasionally, because I have noticed I catch things in print I never caught on the computer screen.

I send the email, lean back in my chair and close my eyes.

Thank You, Lord.

One more book down. As soon as I get her revisions, I'll send it to Joe and then he should be sending me the next book on my docket.

I send Joe a quick email to let him know I just finished it up. He writes back almost immediately, which means he's working late tonight.

Great! Good job, Katie. I know it will be a million times better. I need you in New York on Monday and Tuesday.

I sigh. Oh yay.

By the time I get my shoes on to walk over to Eliza's house, it's a few minutes after six and I now have a Sunday afternoon flight to New York.

I knock on Eliza's door and when she opens it a few seconds later, the most incredible smells come wafting out of the house behind her.

"Oh my goodness," I say, inhaling and closing my eyes. "I can come for dinner anytime you want me."

She grins. "You haven't even tried it yet. Come on in, Ashten should be here in couple of minutes. We need to figure out how to get her to move to this neighborhood, too."

She leads me into the kitchen and I'm amazed at how quickly she's gotten everything set up and homey-feeling. My living room still isn't decorated. And there are definitely boxes floor to ceiling in the guest room closet I haven't unpacked.

"Holy cow, Eliza!" I say, looking around. "Can you come do my house next?"

She grins. "I would love to! I love this kind of stuff. I seriously could spend my entire paycheck at Hobby Lobby."

I have tried to like Hobby Lobby, I honestly have. But every time I walk in there, I feel like I'm about four breaths shy of a panic attack. Too many crafty things, too many breakable things, and too much Christmas in the middle of August.

And I even like Christmas.

"Well, I wasn't kidding. I'll even pay you to do it," I tell her.

She lifts the lid of a huge pot on the stove and steam billows out. She stirs the soup and turns it down.

"What did you make?" I ask, looking over her shoulder.

"It's a chili recipe. But I like my chili with a kick of sweetness, so I added some brown sugar. Oh, and some Worcestershire sauce because, you know, why not?"

I can feel my stomach rumbling. And she sounds like my grandmother with the whole adding this and adding that. I am a stick to the recipe girl. I don't ever deviate from the recipe.

Maybe that's why I've been having a hard time with my life not turning out exactly as I anticipated.

Something to think about on another day.

The oven timer dings right as Eliza's doorbell rings, so she nods me to the door while she slides an oven mitt on her hand. "Can you grab that?" she asks, opening the oven and pulling out a huge pan of cornbread.

Dear goodness, I might just move in here.

I walk back to the front door and open it for Ashten.

"Hi Katie!" she grins. "Hey, don't you live on this street, too?"

I point to my house across the street. "Right there."

"That's so fun! And oh my gosh, it smells like heaven in here." She sets her purse on the couch and we walk into the kitchen together. Eliza is pulling out tiny bowls of sour cream, chives and cheddar cheese and setting them on the counter along with some soup bowls.

"I don't think I've eaten this good since last summer when I was living at home," Ashten says. "And even then, with restaurant hours, you only get to eat when it gets slow and it never gets slow in the summer at Minnie's."

"Well, I hope it tastes good. Thanks for coming to help me eat it!" Eliza grins at us and wipes her hands on a towel. "I'll pray and then we can serve." She ducks her head and closes her eyes. "Jesus, thank you for these friends and for this food and we just pray that it tastes good and no one ends up with salmonella. Amen."

I grin. "Should we be concerned about salmonella?"

"Dude, I went through nursing school. I'm always concerned about salmonella."

Ashten laughs. "You should come work in my class and see what some of my kids bring for lunch. You might be less scared then."

"Likely not. Okay. So, here's the bowls, there are the plates for the cornbread. And I've got lots of fixings for the top of the chili. Katie, start us off."

I pick up a bowl and ladle the steaming chili into it, topping it with cheese, sour cream and chives and I cut myself a healthy slice of cornbread. Eliza has butter, utensils and napkins on the table in the kitchen.

Ashten and Eliza get their chili and cornbread and join me at the table. "So, how's the week been so far?" Eliza asks, buttering her cornbread.

"Good," Ashten nods. "Halloween this weekend."

Eliza sighs. "I hate that holiday. I love most holidays, but I could do without Halloween. Last year, I had these kids who were like three feet tall come to my door dressed like the Grim Reaper. If that doesn't give you nightmares, I don't know what does." She shudders. "Kids grow up too early."

I had totally forgotten about Halloween. I guess I need to go buy some candy sometime in the next two days. I bet we get a lot of trick-or-treaters in this neighborhood. The streets are quiet, the houses are cute and taken care of and most of the people here seem to be either young families or older couples. It's the pick of the litter, as far as streets to trick-or-treat on are concerned.

"How was your week, Katie?"

I shrug. "Normal. I just found out that I have to go to New York next week for two days."

Eliza sighs. "Oh, New York! Can I come with you? I have always heard about New York in the fall!"

I nod. "Sure. Want to know how much my flights were?" I tell her the number and she blanches.

"Or maybe not. I'd like to still eat this month. And, you know, pay the mortgage. Plus, can you imagine the look on Mike's face if I told him I was going to New York City for a couple of days?" She grins. "That almost makes me want to do it."

"You are a terrible sister," I tell her. "And it's not going to be that much fun. This trip is so fast and it's all business. I have a two day meeting that I have to go to. But we should definitely go one of these days for a fun trip."

"I don't know. Your trip this week sounds fun," Ashten says, rolling her eyes.

"It's going to be a blast," I say. "Sitting all day in a freezing cold building arguing with people over what makes a good story. It's going to be great."

"I can tell you what makes a good story," Ashten says. "We just did a Write Your Own Story unit in my classroom. All the kids had to create their own picture book."

"Wow," Eliza nods. "I definitely would have flunked that class."

"You have so much imagination, Eliza. You would have flourished."

She snorts. "I do not have imagination. Please don't mistake my loudness for imagination."

"Your house is beautiful, though!" Ashten waves her hand around the room. "All of this takes imagination."

"Okay, let's look around here." Eliza points to everything Ashten has gestured to. "Pinterest, Pinterest, Pinterest. That wreath idea I stole from my neighbor in St. Louis. Those sconces I found at Target and then copied the idea they had on the box and that little scarecrow thing I got at Hobby Lobby."

I point to the canvas she has on the wall above one of her side tables. "Where did you get that?"

"Some girls at the hospital in St. Louis made it for me when I left." She grins. "They made it by dipping all the disposable stuff we use on a regular basis in paint and then stamping it onto the canvas. You don't even want to know what some of that stuff is."

"Creative and creepy," I say.

"Well, that pretty much describes the nurses I left."

Ashten grins. "How would you describe the nurses here?"

Eliza shrugs. "Things are totally different here. In St. Louis, there are a lot of hospitals and people have a lot of different options when it comes to where they are going to get their hospital care. Here, people have just a few options and so I feel like we are packed all day long. I've barely talked to a lot of my coworkers because we are just scrub-covered blurs passing each other in the hallway." She eats a bite of chili. "Speaking of which, let's talk about that Bible study thing again."

"'Speaking of which'?" Ashten grins. "How was that a 'speaking of which'?"

Eliza shrugs. "I don't know. I thought about it right then."

"Your brain activity is like a squirrel's while they are gathering nuts for the winter," I tell her.

Ashten laughs.

Eliza shrugs again. "You guys can make fun of me all you want. You have no idea what kind of job perk it is to be a nurse who is able to think of twelve different things at the same time."

"We didn't say it wasn't a perk," Ashten says. "I just think it's funny. I would literally go crazy if my brain worked like that."

I am scraping the bottom of my bowl and debating seconds. "Eliza, that was the best chili I've ever had," I tell her. "Don't tell my mother I said that."

"Seriously," Ashten nods. "You should quit nursing and be a chef."

"Yeah, but the job satisfaction rate would be a lot lower for me," Eliza says. "Thanks, guys. Glad you liked it. Now, are you guys still thinking this Bible study thing is a good idea?"

I nod. "Most definitely. I need a good Bible study." And some actual accountability. Lately, it's been too easy to turn on Netflix rather than read my Bible.

Ashten is nodding. "I'm on board, too."

"Great! I was thinking we could do First John."

I grin. "That's what I came up with, too."

"Ashten? Any rebuttal?"

Ashten shakes her head. "I like First John."

"First John it is. How do we want to do this? Should we find a study on it or should we all just kind of read through it and discuss it? What do you think?"

We debate the pros and cons of both and end up deciding to spend the first few weeks reading through it ourselves and discussing it. Then we might possibly find a study to do on it. We are going to meet on Wednesday nights at my house, assuming I'm in town.

"So, we can start next week," Eliza says.

"Sounds good to me," I nod.

"Me, too," Ashten says.

I leave Eliza's house at nine o'clock, stuffed full of chili, cornbread and some sort of bar that was basically a brownie mixed with a chocolate chip cookie. I'm fairly certain it will be served in heaven.

Ashten unlocks her car as I walk across the street. "Dude, I am jealous of this right now," she says, waving to my house.

I get one of those ideas that formulates in my brain only seconds before it's coming out of my mouth. "You should move in here with me," I tell her.

She looks at me. "Seriously?"

I'm nodding even as I'm thinking through the plan. I work from home, but she's not home during my work hours. I travel a ton and it would be great to know my house wasn't sitting there vacant while I'm gone. And, she moves back in with her family during the summer, so this way, all her stuff could just stay here and she wouldn't have to be moving in and out of apartments every year.

It totally makes sense to me. Plus, honestly, I could really use the company.

"Yes," I say. "Here, you should just come look at it really quick so you can decide."

She closes her car door and follows me across the street.

Compared to Eliza's fully decorated house, my house looks terribly bare and empty. I had the house painted before I moved in, but that's basically all that has been done to it. I haven't hung anything on the wall, and I haven't put up any real fall decorations. I do have a candle on the fireplace mantel.

It's pumpkin scented.

Surely that counts for something.

It's a three bedroom house, which is way too big for what I need. I think I have stepped in the guest room three times since I moved in. And that was just to get stuff out of the boxes I keep in the closet.

I show her around the living room and the kitchen. Then I take her down the hallway to the guest room.

"So, this is my guest room," I tell her. "It comes with all the furniture."

She grins. I didn't have enough furniture for the guest room and I haven't had the time or desire to go spend money for furniture to put in here, so it's basically just an empty room. I had originally thought of making it a workout room, but I do everything else at home, so it's better to join a gym and see the general public every so often.

"I don't know," Ashten says, slowly. "I mean, are you sure, Katie? This would be absolutely wonderful, but I really don't want to impose on your space."

"Ashten, you'll be at work all day and I would love the company at night."

She looks at the room again and I show her the bathroom just across the hallway. It's small but functional.

"The room and bathroom aren't much," I tell her.

"Katie, they're beautiful. Don't downplay it. I'm just deciding if I would make you crazy if I lived here." She smiles at me. "Being friends with someone is one thing. Living with them is a totally different animal. I'm not sure it's even in the same species."

"I think it could work really well. Just think about it and let me know, okay? Plus, if you got on my nerves too much, I could just kick you over to Eliza's for a few hours."

She grins. "True." She nods. "I'll think on it."

"When is your lease up on your apartment?"

"The end of the month."

"Ashten, that's like six days."

She shrugs. "I just do month to month since I move out every summer. I've been at this same apartment complex every school year, so they just keep my lease and let me move back in to an available apartment when August rolls around."

"That's nice of them."

"Super nice." She looks at her watch, yawning. "Well, I'm going to go. I have to get through a few progress reports before I go to bed tonight and I have to be up early for a staff meeting in the morning before school."

I nod. "Sounds good. Just let me know."

"Oh, I definitely will."

CHAPTER *Eleven*

I knock on Gram's door at six o'clock on Friday night. This week, I made sure I actually retouched my makeup and tried to tame my hair for dinner since we had our surprise guest last week. Though, I doubt he noticed my flyaway hair since he was looking at his cell phone so much.

Here's my friendly PSA for all men who are single: If you are wanting to find a girl, you can start by putting your phone away. Possibly even turning it off. Despite what people may tell you, I don't think that Mr. Darcy would have ever texted Elizabeth.

Texting is not romantic.

Gram opens the door and smiles at me. "Well, don't you look all lovely?" she says, letting me in.

"Well, based on last week, it seems that our Friday night dinners have become more than just a grandmother and her granddaughter affair," I say, closing and locking the door behind me.

Gram rolls her eyes. "You are just like your mother. So prone to overreact when I make the slightest move to help you guys find the right man. You don't see her complaining now."

I look at Gram. "Wait, you fixed up Mom and Dad? I thought they met at church."

"Honey, how do you think they met at church? Your dad, bless his heart, was so dense he couldn't even see a brick wall in front of him back then, much less a beautiful girl."

"So, you saw this dense man and thought he would be the perfect son-in-law for you?"

Gram pats my arm. "The odds of me being around when you are trying to find your future sons' wives are not good, so let me just say this now." She pauses and looks at me seriously. "The more malleable the better." Then she pats my arm and walks into the kitchen.

"I'm not sure that's totally Biblical," I say, following her.

"Not being malleable in your beliefs, honey. Just in the way you live your life. Just think for a minute about your dad and how he eats his dinner."

I don't remember anything particularly weird about how my father eats.

Gram nods. "See? Exactly. Before he started dating your mother, the man barely used a utensil correctly. Now, he can set the table properly, cut his steak properly and hold a fork the right way."

I grin. "Surely he wasn't that bad, Gram."

"I once saw him try to use the wrong side of a fork, Katie."

"Gram."

"To eat spaghetti. I swear to you on my aged life."

I laugh.

Gram's kitchen is empty so it appears that I wasted the dab of lipstick and the reapplication of eye shadow. I settle onto the barstool in the kitchen feeling a weird mix of relief and disappointment, which is just proof right there that I have reached a new level of desperation.

I can't even tell you how many times I've been told I need to just get out there and meet people and put myself in different places and different social circles. Other than ending up close to being broke from all the extra activities and food I was paying for, I never saw a difference. Sure, I met different people but I would say that eighty percent of the men I met were already with someone, fifteen percent weren't looking and had no plans to ever be looking and the five percent who were trying to meet a girl were just a sad lot.

I even went to a church one time in New York that was known for its freakishly large amount of single men.

To put it the way one of my coworkers at the time said it, the odds were good but the goods were odd.

Really odd.

Here's the thing: If you are over the age of three and still wearing one piece footed pajamas to bed, you should just keep that information to yourself. I don't really care how cold it gets at night in your apartment or whether or not they were a Star Wars character.

Gram's kitchen, as per normal, smells amazing and she is ladling some sort of white potato soup into two bowls.

"What did you make, Gram?"

"Sausage, potato and corn chowder. My mama used to make this and always swore that it would keep you warm until the tulips bloomed again."

I smile. I never met my great-grandmother, but I love hearing stories about the family tree. Gram's mother was a first generation American. Her parents immigrated here from Sweden and my great-grandmother was born exactly six months to the day after they first stepped foot on American soil.

Anytime Gram tells that story, she has to take a moment of silence to commemorate her great-grandmother's extreme morning sickness on board the boat on her way to America.

Gram's phone rings and she answers it, handing me an oven mitt and nodding to the oven.

"Hello?"

I open the oven door and there's a loaf of Gram's homemade honey oat bread inside.

I swear, I should just give my house to Ashten and move in here with Gram. I'm sure she gets lonely.

Actually, Gram has more lunch dates and dinner dates and activities in a normal week than almost anyone I know. She's rarely home. I don't know how she has the time to prepare Friday night dinners.

"Mm. Oh yes, honey, I understand. No, you just come on over. Yes, I'm sure. Mm-hmm. See you shortly."

She hangs up the phone and looks at the bread. "Is it done?" she asks me.

"I don't know. How do you tell?"

She points to the top. "The color looks good, but you also want to lightly rap on the top with your knuckles." She does and a slight hollow sound echoes back, making her smile. "Perfectly done. Thank you for getting it out."

"Sure. Everything okay?"

"We're going to have an extra guest tonight," Gram says, pulling another bowl from the cabinet.

I smirk. "See? I knew it."

"Sadly, it's not a man of marriageable age and financial security. It's Olive Klein, one of my friends. I think you may have met her at the wedding."

I nod. "She's nice."

"She's too nice. People just walk all over her because she's so nice, but you didn't hear that from me."

I grin. "Yes, ma'am."

"Not that I'm saying you shouldn't be nice," Gram says. "You should also know when people have stopped being nice and started being takers all the time from you. Olive is the sweetest, most generous soul on the planet and everyone around her knows it." Gram shakes her head. "You don't find a line of Girl Scouts outside my front door at cookie time. We'll have to eat in the dining room again, honey, unless we're going to make Olive stand to eat and that's pretty much impossible with soup."

I hide my smile as I carry the bowls to the dining room table. I'm not sure Gram knows exactly how sweet and generous she is.

Olive arrives a couple of minutes later. "Oh, Mabel, you didn't tell me you had company tonight," she says, as soon as she walks in and sees me.

"Psh," Gram says, closing the door. "It's my granddaughter, Olive. She's not company, she's family."

"I know, but I hate to interrupt. I know how much you treasure this time with your sweet girl."

Something warm and sweet like the melting honey dripping off the crust on the honey oat bread blossoms deep in my stomach. Gram's not the most sappy and sentimental, so hearing that she really does enjoy our time together that much means a lot.

Gram waves a hand. "I'm still having time with her and we've already served you a bowl of chowder. Did you bring your medicine?"

Olive nods and reaches in her purse.

"Olive can't handle lactose," Gram tells me.

"It messes up my digestion something awful," Olive says, shaking out two pills into her hand. She sits at the table, swallowing the pills with a drink of her water beside her bowl. "But your grandmother's soup is just too good not to eat."

"I agree," I nod.

"Has she made you her clam chowder yet?"

I shake my head.

"Legendary," Olive declares.

Gram waves her hand again. "Listen to you, going on. Let's pray for humility before it all goes to my head."

I grin and close my eyes.

Gram prays a short, sweet prayer. She goes in the kitchen, coming back out with a cutting board and a bread knife.

Olive takes a swallow of Gram's chowder and just shakes her head. "Amazing," she says.

"Thank you. Now. Perhaps you can shed some light on my granddaughter's situation over here," Gram says.

I look up. "What situation?" I wasn't aware that I had a situation.

"Singleness, honey. Do you have any advice for her, Olive?"

Olive shakes her head at me. "Oh no, Mabel. I don't get involved in these matters of the heart. You should have invited Frieda over for chowder." Olive looks at me. "I'm surprised Frieda hasn't already married you off. Frieda only needs to talk to someone for about six minutes usually before she finds the right person for them. It's a bit of a running joke now at church."

"Well, she wasn't too successful with her own grandchild, either," Gram says.

"I mean, there were different issues at play there," Olive says, taking the slice of bread Gram offers her with a murmured thanks. "Specifically, there were some hair issues."

Gram rolls her eyes. "There weren't hair issues. Long hair is back in style for men, Olive."

"It's just not right. It's not Biblical."

"What about Samson?" Gram retorts.

"Katie, you just hold out for a good man," Olive says to me, patting my left hand and ignoring Gram. "You wait for the perfect man, someone who loves you, respects you, and who knows the value of a good barber."

I nod, most likely failing at hiding my grin. "Yes, ma'am."

I load my carry-on suitcase into the trunk and close it, looking over the car at Eliza. "Are you sure you don't mind taking me to the airport?" I ask her again.

"Katie, sheesh. I'm the one who offered to take you! Just say thank you, stop asking and get in the car."

"Thank you."

"You're welcome. Get in the car," she says again.

I slide into the passenger seat of her Toyota Corolla. "This is nice," I tell her.

"Thanks. It was my gift to myself for holding a grown up job for a whole year." She pats the steering wheel as she turns the ignition. "Robby has been with me through thick and thin. And by that I am referring to the fluids that have seeped into my scrubs I'm wearing as I drive home every day."

I can feel my nose wrinkling up and I scoot a little farther away from Eliza and closer to my door. "Um, gross."

"Nursing is not for the faint of heart, my friend."

"Or the faint of stomach."

"Right."

"Which I am, so could we keep the fluid talk to a minimum?" I am gagging now. Even the word *fluid* just sounds disgusting.

Eliza grins over at me as she leaves our neighborhood. "So Ashten told me that you asked her to move in."

I nod. "She might as well. It would save us both some money. And she wouldn't have to keep moving in and out of her apartment every fall."

"I think it's a great idea! I would love to have you both across the street. Though, she works so much that we would probably never see her. You know, I always thought teachers had a cushy job until I actually talked to one."

"You're telling me." I double check that I have my boarding pass and my driver's license in my wallet. "So, did she tell you whether or not she's thinking of moving in?" I ask.

Eliza shrugs. "She said she was thinking and praying about it, but that she didn't know yet. She said would have an answer, though, by the time you got home Tuesday night."

"Well, I hope so. Her lease is up at the end of the month."

Eliza waves a hand. "Yeah, but she said it's on like this auto-renewal thing."

"Still. Doesn't the apartment complex require some sort of advance notice?"

"I have no idea. Maybe she has a really good relationship with them. I don't know. I haven't lived in an apartment in five years and even then, I only lived in one with another girl for six months before we couldn't stand it anymore and found a rental house that cost about fifty bucks more a month. I would have spent even more than that, though. You can't put a price on your own walls and the ability to load groceries directly into your house."

"Amen, sister."

We pull up to the airport a few minutes later and I climb out, bending down and smiling at Eliza. "Thanks for the ride."

"Sure thing! Have a safe trip. What time do you land on Tuesday?"

I'm catching the late flight coming home so I don't have to fly out Wednesday morning. "Late. Eleven, I think. I can get a cab to get me."

Eliza rolls her eyes. "That would be ridiculous. I'll pick you up. Text me your flight information. I don't work Wednesday, so I'm just going to be sleeping in that morning anyway. I'll be well rested."

"If you're sure." I feel totally guilty right now. Maybe I'm just not used to people doing things for me just for the sake of it, but I hate making her come all the way out here in the middle of the night.

"Don't worry about it. Like I said earlier, I wouldn't offer if I didn't want to do it." She pushes a button and pops the trunk so I can get my suitcase out. "Have a safe flight, Katie!"

"Thanks again, Eliza."

"See you on Tuesday night."

I close her passenger door and wave as she drives off. I walk through the double automatic doors and head straight for the gates. I just brought a carry-on suitcase, so I get to bypass all the lines, which aren't bad today. Most of the people traveling today are business people, probably heading out for morning meetings like I am.

I find my gate, stop and buy a magazine to read on the plane that claims it has the top twenty "must have" outfits of the Christmas season. I usually try to make sure I've got a novel uploaded on an app on my phone, but sometimes it's nice to read something with a lot of pictures that I'm not constantly editing in my mind.

We board the plane and I end up getting an aisle seat on a row by myself. The best kind of flight.

The captain comes on over the intercom system. "Good afternoon, ladies and gentlemen, this is your captain speaking. Looking like a quick trip to St. Louis today. Just sit back and enjoy your flight."

I lean back and close my eyes. This leg of the trip is only a twenty minute flight. Barely long enough to get to cruising altitude.

We land in St. Louis, I board my flight to La Guardia and this flight is completely full. I end up shoved against the window, with an obnoxiously loud, very large man sitting next to me. He's holding two of those miniature alcoholic drink bottles. He orders more every ten minutes and by the time we land, I'm convinced he's going to need a wheelchair escort off the plane.

But everyone in the ten foot radius around him knows all about this man, his career that is going nowhere and that he can't figure out why his relationships always end badly.

I wish my magazine had come with noise canceling headphones.

At one point, I tried to actually converse with him and maybe talk to him about Jesus, but I have a feeling he was already drinking for awhile before he got on the plane. There was no way anything I was going to say was going to matter at that point.

It was a long flight, to say the least.

By the time I get out of the taxi at the hotel, I am exhausted and I feel disgusting. I head straight up the elevator,

find my room, lock the door behind me and go directly to the shower. I get out, debate about putting on clothes and going back out for dinner and just decide to get room service in my pajamas.

I call in the order and twenty minutes later, they are knocking at my door with the tray. I carry it in the room, climb up on the bed and turn the TV to a rerun of a home renovation show that I've seen before, but it's quiet and mindless.

I set the tray back outside the door and I'm back in bed asleep before the show is even over.

CHAPTER *Twelve*

I arrive at the office a few minutes early for the meeting. Joe is in his office, furiously typing away on his computer.

"Knock, knock," I say, rapping lightly on his open door.

He looks up and grins. "Hey there, Katie. Give me just a minute. Hey, I think we had bagels delivered today. I heard there were pumpkin spice ones with some sort of pumpkin chocolate cream cheese, so if you want one, you might want to get in there early."

"Thanks!" I head over to the conference room and a girl in a black polo shirt with a black baseball cap is unloading trays of bagels and cream cheese onto the long counter beside the conference table.

"Hey," she says to me.

"Hi. I heard you brought pumpkin bagels."

She grins. "Pumpkin cranberry. Word of the wise, though, don't slather them with the pumpkin cream cheese unless you're like the biggest gourd fan in the world. Personally, I can't do that much pumpkin. But the cinnamon cream cheese on one of those is pretty much amazing."

"Thanks for the tip," I nod.

"No problem. You guys have a good meeting." She packs up her boxes and leaves, whistling.

One of the things I love about this area of the city is how you are never at a shortage for one of the world's best bakeries.

People start trickling in, most going straight for the bagels. I finish spreading the cinnamon cream cheese spread over my pumpkin bagel and sit at the conference table in the spot I always sit.

"Hi Katie." Maggie sits down beside me and I smile over at her. Maggie was one of the first people I met when I started working at Townsend and Mitchell. She's a couple of years older than my mom, she has a few grandkids and she likes to channel Mrs. Bennet. Her whole mission in life when I lived here was to find me a husband.

Obviously, it wasn't a super successful mission.

They could probably make a film about it and put it in the litany of *Mission Impossible* movies. What are they on now? Seven? Twelve? Thirty-eight? And how is it that Tom Cruise never ages through any of them?

Regardless.

"Went with the pumpkin, I see," Maggie says, nodding to the plastic plate in front of me.

"Had to. It's the end of October. I think something terrible happens to you if you don't eat pumpkin in the month of October."

"Like what?"

I shrug. "I don't know, but with Halloween and all those creepy people ringing my doorbell, I didn't want to find out."

She laughs. "I've missed you around here, Katie. Oh hey, speaking of which, I have someone you need to meet!"

I look at my watch. So, it took Maggie about two and a half minutes before she started matchmaking.

She's showing some restraint today.

"Oh really?" I ask.

"You really could put some enthusiasm in your voice, Katie."

"Maggie, I've heard this before and it never works out. And now my grandmother is also setting me up in Carrington Springs and I'm just honestly getting a little tired of it."

Not even necessarily tired of the matchmaking, but more tired of the lack of success. I mean, they say that there is someone out there for everyone. I've met some people who were just flat out weird and they are now married with kids.

Maybe I'm weirder than I thought I was, but how are they married and I'm still over here sitting at tables for one?

Maggie brushes off my comments. "Oh, please. You know you want to get married."

"I didn't say that I didn't want to get married, Maggie."

"Well, good! Because this guy is *perfect*."

I can't even remember how many times Maggie has told me this phrase over the years. One time, she was going on and on about some random man she'd met at a coffeehouse, who was apparently the most attractive man in New York. He was perfect for me, at least he was until she found out he was married with three kids, but didn't wear a ring because he found it easier to get discounts on his coffee without it.

If that is perfect for me, I'd rather stay single.

"Maggie."

"No, I'm serious, Katie."

"You were serious the last time, too. Remember? With that waiter guy from the Bronx?"

"I was only half-serious then."

"Or what about the stockbroker guy who thought he'd broken his leg on our blind date?"

Maggie grins. "But think about the story you got from that one."

I shake my head. The guy stepped weird off a curb and immediately sank to the sidewalk, grabbing his leg and shouting, "My leg! It's broken! My leg is broken! Someone call an ambulance!"

Actually, he'd just popped his knee somehow and after a two hour wait in the emergency room, we found out he just needed to walk it off, basically.

That was one of those dates I was too embarrassed to even write my own mother about.

Maggie swallows a bite of her own pumpkin bagel. "Anyway, this one is it. I'll stake my life on it."

"Your life was already staked on Broken Leg."

"My second life, then. I knew you were coming in town, so I arranged for you guys to have dinner tonight at Serendipity's."

"Seriously?" I can't decide if I'm frustrated or if I'm excited for one of their legendary frozen hot chocolates. Though, Serendipity's also equals an incredibly long wait.

"And I got you reservations, so don't even worry about having to make small talk in that ridiculously tiny foyer."

I shake my head. "We'll see how your second life turns out."

"Trust me. You will love him. Like, literally. And I require at least a guest book attendant position when you marry this man, preferably a bridesmaid. I look great in fuchsia, in case you were wondering."

I try and fail at not laughing.

Maggie grins at me. "Miss having you around here, Katie," she says again.

I miss being around Maggie, too.

Our meeting ends at five-thirty and by the time I get out of the taxi at Serendipity 3, it's almost six-fifteen. I considered walking, but the forty-five degree sunny morning we had turned into a thirty-something degree windy night.

I'm getting soft in Missouri. Three months ago, I would have walked the four and a half blocks.

I get to the restaurant and look around the people shivering outside while they wait. No men by themselves. I open the door and the lobby is packed with people and it's incredibly loud inside.

There is no way I'm going to find him in this mess. I don't even know what he looks like other than he should be alone. Maggie wasn't the most detailed with her description of him.

"He's like this super attractive mix of that doctor on that one TV show that got cancelled and moved to Netflix and the man in that Sylvester Stallone movie," she told me.

I have no idea what she was talking about. The only Stallone movie I've ever seen was *Rocky* and it wasn't life changing enough to watch more than once, nor was it convincing of his talent enough to make me want to watch more of his movies.

The Italian Stallion just wasn't my type, I guess.

"McCoy, party of two!" the hostess yells out into the crowd.

Well, that's me, but I'm not seeing the other part of my party of two. I approach the hostess and she just looks at me.

"Is your entire party here?" she asks.

"Um," I start, and then I feel a tap on my shoulder.

I look over and there's a man standing there who I wouldn't call super attractive but he's also not incredibly unattractive. He's about five or six inches taller than me and wearing black dress pants and a white button-down shirt under a gray, double-breasted wool coat. He's got short, blond-ish hair and he's clean shaven.

Basically, he looks like every other business man walking the streets of New York right now.

"Katie?"

I nod. Maggie had told me his name and that's about all I know about him, though based on his outfit, I can pretty much guarantee that he's some sort of want-to-be CEO.

"J.T.?" I ask.

He nods and the hostess looks at us impatiently. "McCoy, party of two?" she says again.

"We're both here," J.T. says.

As a rule, I've never been a fan of initial names. Why can't you just go by your actual name? Are you embarrassed of it? Is it too long? Too short? Too childish? Or are you just a fan of punctuation in your name?

We follow the hostess and she leads us upstairs where it is, thankfully, so much quieter.

I guess it could be both good and bad that it's so much quieter. On the one hand, we can actually hear what the other person is saying when we are telling each other about ourselves. On the other hand, if we don't like what we hear, there's not a lot of distraction to minimize the awkwardness.

I hate blind dates.

The hostess sets two menus at a tiny table tucked around the corner from the stairs. We sit down and here comes the part that I really hate: the opening lines.

You know how they say the first few sentences of a book are the most important? I sort of feel that way on dates, too.

"So, J.T. Does that stand for something?" I ask and then immediately feel like a moron because of course it stands for something. You don't just name your kid initials.

Do you?

J.T. nods. "My name is Justin Tyler Williams."

"You just prefer J.T.?"

"My dad is also Justin. So is my grandfather. It got confusing when I was growing up."

"Oh." I guess that kind of makes sense, but maybe you should find a new name instead of just recycling the same names over and over again.

J.T. smiles at me. It's a nice smile. "So, Maggie tells me that you're a freelance editor?"

I nod. "I actually live in Carrington Springs, Missouri," I tell him. "I just travel here a few times a month."

He nods. "Very nice. Sometimes I think it would be nice not to live in the city anymore, but work and all its incentives make it hard to leave."

"I do miss the coffee houses," I tell him.

He smiles. "I would imagine Missouri coffee isn't exactly the same."

"Not exactly."

A waitress comes by with two glasses of water for us. "Are you ready to order?" she asks us.

J.T. orders a hamburger with all the fixings and I order the tortellini primavera. Everyone knows the main reason to come to Serendipity's is for dessert, so I always try to order something I can immediately put half of in a to-go box and save for later.

Pasta saves way better than burgers.

"So, tell me about yourself," J.T. says after the waitress leaves.

Ah, The Opening. I've never understood this statement. What exactly do they want to know? There is so much to someone beyond what they can tell you. Even if they could, it would take way longer than what the typical person wants to listen to.

I shrug. "Well, I'm Katie. I'm an editor. Like I said, I live in Missouri. I have dinner with my grandmother once a week. I'm a

Christian." I shrug again. There isn't a lot left that I would tell this random stranger about myself.

He smiles again. "That's great. I'm a Christian, too. It's been tough trying to find a good church in Manhattan. I grew up in the Bible belt, kind of where you moved to, actually, and it's a lot different here."

I nod. "I lived here for a few years before I moved to Missouri."

"Did you grow up there?"

I shake my head. "No, but my mom did. And my grandmother is still there. I looked at moving back to my hometown, but Gram could use the company and honestly, Carrington Springs is a really cute little town. It's got a huge medical community. Lots of farmland. Lots of good restaurants. Where did you grow up?" He doesn't have the hard New York accent or mannerisms, so I knew he wasn't from around here even before he mentioned it.

"Tennessee, actually. I know where Carrington Springs is. I think my dad went there for a heart procedure a few years back. Right on the Mississippi River?"

I nod. "That's it."

"Very cool."

"Does your family still live in Tennessee?"

J.T. nods. "My dad does. My mom moved to Oregon a few years ago."

Broken home. I think of my own parents and their strong marriage and just feel a pricking in my soul.

Jesus, how do you handle my constant complaints in the face of other people's suffering?

"I'm sorry," I tell him and he shrugs.

"You know, it happens. And they are much happier apart than they ever were together. It makes the holidays hard, but so does all the snow New York gets, so I haven't actually made it back for Christmas in a long time." He fiddles with his napkin. "Kind of makes it easier."

We talk until the food comes. I find out he's got an older sister who is married with two kids. She still lives in Tennessee. He's planning on spending Christmas with them.

We talk through dinner and, surprisingly, it's actually kind of nice. He seems to be somewhat normal, which is amazing considering Maggie's track record. He's got a nice smile and his brownish-hazel eyes seem kind. He talks about his family a lot and rarely mentions work.

In this city, that's a rare thing.

We both order a frozen hot chocolate, which is crazy because there's no way I can finish a whole one of these by myself. I've seen couples eating it together and some of them still haven't finished it.

But it's also one of those weird things where I don't know him well enough to share a dessert. Sharing a dessert is one of those things that seems kind of intimate and I'm not sure why.

Too many chick-flicks, probably.

He manages to finish all of it, along with his burger. The man is what I would call on the thinner side, so either he hasn't eaten all day or he's got a metabolism like an NCAA athlete. I barely get to what I might consider the halfway point of my frozen hot chocolate and I only ate half my dinner. I've got the rest in a box on the table beside me.

"Can I get you guys anything else?" The waitress is standing by our table, holding our check, so she obviously knows our answer.

"No, thank you," J.T. says.

"Well, I hope you enjoyed your dinner. Come see us again soon."

This is the sign that you know you've adapted to New York is when the waiters start treating you like locals. I distinctly remember the first time I experienced it. I'd been living here for almost six months and it was the first time I wasn't asked where I was visiting from.

"Oh, I can get my meal," I say to J.T. as he pulls a gold Visa card out of his wallet.

"No, no. I've got this."

What is the right protocol in this situation? Do I insist in demanding my half of the check? Is it proper etiquette to let the man pay even if it was a blind date and I didn't finish all my food? Because, technically, thanks to the mini fridge in my hotel room, he's now paying for lunch tomorrow, too.

But, I also don't want to insult him and isn't there like some man code about paying for things on a date? So, maybe I shouldn't insist on the check?

I don't know what to do. The last guy I went on a blind date with had "broken" his leg way before we ever made it to dinner.

I wiggle my spoon around in the quickly melting frozen hot chocolate leftovers. "Thank you, J.T.," I say quietly.

"No problem. This was really fun." He looks up at me, smiles and I know he really means it. "When are you in town again?"

I shake my head. "I'm not sure. I don't have another trip scheduled right now. But it's been about every three weeks."

He nods. "Well, please let me know next time you're in town. I would really like to get dinner with you again."

We stand from the table and he helps me with my coat.

Here's the thing: I've never had anyone help me with my coat before. So, I basically end up punching him in the eye while I'm trying to get my sleeve on.

"Oh my gosh!" I say and I can feel my cheeks turning totally red. "I am so sorry! Are you okay?"

He's rubbing his eye, but he's half-smiling. "I'm fine. That's quite the right hook you've got."

"I'm so sorry."

He grins. "You're fine. Let's go. Where are you staying?"

I tell him the name of the hotel right beside work and he nods. "I have to go that way too," J.T. says. "Would you like to walk with me? It's not that far."

I nod.

We step out of the warm restaurant and a frigid breeze straight from the depths of Canada hits us right in the face.

It's times like this that make me wish I didn't care as much about style as I do. I am dying for a pair of long underwear instead of the super cute silky top I have on under my coat. I think the cold is actually weaving into the fibers of my shirt.

I wonder if you can get frostbite from a silk shirt.

J.T. is talking as we are walking the couple of blocks back to my hotel and I'm not sure how he's able to keep his teeth from chattering.

"You doing okay?" he asks me as we cross the street.

"Hmm? Yeah, I'm f-f-fine," I say and pull my coat closer around me.

J.T. is immediately apologetic. "I'm so sorry. It is really cold right now. Maybe we should just get a cab."

"No, no. I'm good," I say, trying my best to control my shivering. "It's crazy how much colder it is here than in Missouri."

"I'm sure. Let's get a cab."

"J.T., that would be ridiculous for three blocks. I would be laughed out of New York."

"I've heard being laughed out of a city is cheaper than flying, though," he says, grinning at me and I laugh through the shivers.

We get to the hotel and he comes into the lobby with me. It is toasty warm inside and I can smell the coffee from the coffeehouse inside the lobby. They apparently proudly brew Starbucks.

I look at the fairly empty lobby and over at J.T., who doesn't seem like he's in a huge hurry to leave. "Want some coffee?" I ask him and he immediately smiles.

I'll take that as a yes.

CHAPTER *Thirteen*

Eliza is waiting for me when I finally walk out of the airport doors by the baggage claim at eleven-fifteen on Tuesday night.

"Hey," she says, grinning. She's wearing leggings, UGG boots and a sweatshirt and she's got her hair up in a sloppy bun with one of those elastic headbands holding back her bangs.

I could never pull off this look. I would look like some sort of modern day version of that Feed the Birds lady on *Mary Poppins*. Eliza looks adorable and Pinterest worthy.

"Thank you so much again for picking me up." I climb into the car and she waves a hand.

"Good night, Katie, cut it out already. Trust me, I know you're thankful and I have ninety-six texts from you to prove it."

"I did not text you ninety-six times."

"Fine. Eighty-four."

I smile.

She looks over at me. "So, how was the Big Apple?"

"Cold."

"I bet. I heard on the news that a big storm was expected there tonight and tomorrow. I'm glad your plane made it out before then."

"Me too." I've been in New York snowstorms before.

Though, getting stuck in New York wouldn't have been so bad.

"What?" Eliza asks, looking over at me as she merges onto the road.

"What what?" I ask her.

"You just had a weird look on your face." She looks at me again. "Dude, you totally met someone in New York, didn't you?"

I sigh. She can read me way too well considering the short amount of time we've been friends. "Seriously, what are the odds of that?"

"Pretty good, if you can believe the movies! So, where did you meet him? On top of the Empire State Building?"

"I haven't even said there is someone yet!"

Part of me wants to tell her about J.T. and part of me wants to keep him quiet. You never know if something is going to work out. And there's several thousand miles between us.

And as much as I liked talking to him, I just didn't get a lot of...

I don't know the word for it.

"So tell me about him," Eliza persists.

I rub my forehead. "Okay, I did meet someone."

"Ha! I knew it." She does a little victory fist pump into the air. "So? Dish! What is he like? Tall or short? Cute or ugly? How did you meet him?"

"One of the editors I used to work with set me up on a blind date while I was out there."

"No kidding?" Eliza grins over at me. "So, blind dates can actually work, huh?"

"They haven't for me up until now," I tell her. "Everyone I've ever been set up with is just weird. Or totally not my type." I don't even bother telling her about the broken leg guy.

"Yeah, same here. So? What was he like?"

I think about J.T. "I mean, he seems normal."

"Normal? That's it?"

I look over at her. "What do you mean?"

"I mean, where are the fireworks? The cutesy smiles when you are talking about him? The little giggles? The gushing over how cute he is?" Eliza rolls her eyes. "This is like the worst 'I met someone' story I've ever heard."

"Sorry."

"You don't have to apologize. So, were there fireworks?"

I shift back in my seat. "I mean, not really." We talked for another hour about just random stuff after we got our coffee at my hotel. I never noticed any fireworks, but it wasn't terrible, either.

And he never looked at his phone.

So, that's something. Right?

"So, tell me more. What does he look like? And is he a Christian?"

"Yes to the Christian. He's a little bit taller than me. He looks like a New York business guy."

Eliza shrugs. "Like what? Tom Hanks in *You've Got Mail*?"

"Kind of, yeah. Except not really like Tom Hanks."

"So, he looks like Tom Hanks, but he doesn't."

"Right."

She laughs. "Seriously, Katie, I'm going to enroll you in classes on how to dish about men. This is the most painful thing I've ever experienced."

I grin, rubbing my cheek. "Sorry."

"Stop apologizing."

We pull onto our street and Eliza parks in her driveway. She pulls the keys out of the ignition and smiles to me. "Well, I'm glad you met someone."

"Eliza, do you ever worry that maybe you've just been too picky?" I ask suddenly. I wasn't even planning on talking about this, especially considering how late it already is, but I just can't help it.

No, there weren't fireworks with J.T. But, maybe my definition of fireworks isn't even based on reality. Maybe it's totally based on something I've read in books or seen in movies and it doesn't even happen in real life. What if love in real life is just finding someone who fits your definition of normal and is someone who you know will be there through the years?

Eliza angles toward me a little bit and shakes her head. "I mean, no. But you haven't met any of my ex-boyfriends," she grins.

"True. What about that guy who keeps proposing to you?"

"Landon?" She starts laughing. "Yeah. It's never going to happen."

"Why not?"

She shrugs. "I just know it's never going to happen. It's nothing against him. He's a great guy. Strong Christian, actually kind of cute. But there's just no spark, you know?"

"That's kind of my point," I say. "What if we are looking for this thing that doesn't exist? I mean, maybe it's like that story of the guy in the house by the river that's flooding and he prays for God to save him."

Eliza frowns at me. "What?"

"You haven't heard that story?"

"I have no idea what you are talking about. You're comparing singleness to dying in a flood?"

I laugh. "No, there's just this story that made the email circular that was about this guy who lives in this house by the river. So, the river is flooding and he prays for God to rescue him and this guy comes by in a police car and offers him a ride. The man turns it down because he's waiting for God to save him. So then it floods some more and a boat comes by and offers him a ride. He turns it down again because God is going to save him. So, it's still flooding and he has to climb up on top of his roof to escape the water and a helicopter comes by and offers him a ride and—"

"Let me guess."

I nod. "He again turns it down so God can save him."

Eliza shakes her head. "Sounds like kind of a dense guy. Not unlike a few of the guys I've dated." She grins. "So what happened?"

"He drowns."

"You are totally comparing singleness to drowning in a flood!"

"No, he drowns and goes to heaven. When he asks God why He didn't save him, God says, 'I sent you the police car, the boat and the helicopter! What more did you want me to do?'"

Eliza just looks at me, her confused face illuminated by the porch lights on her house. "I don't get it. The moral of the story is to stay away from men who are dumb and won't protect you if your house is flooding?"

I laugh. "The point of the story was that God answered this guy's prayers, but he wasn't open to the way He was answering them."

"So, you think that God might be answering your prayers by having you meet this guy, even though you didn't have any attraction to him."

"I'm just wondering if sparks are overrated."

Eliza looks at me for a few minutes and then looks out the windshield. "Katie, the only person who ever said that ended up with Mr. Collins. And I don't know about you, but I'd rather not be counting on him to do something if our house was flooding."

I don't think she totally understood the point of my story.

Wednesday morning, I break my only code about working at home and start work in my pajamas. It's already nine o'clock and I'm barely up and moving, which isn't good, because that means it's already eleven in New York.

I bet my email inbox is overflowing.

By the time I got inside my house last night and got ready for bed, it was past midnight. Then, I kept thinking about Eliza's comment on Mr. Collins and I couldn't fall asleep.

She basically thought I was Charlotte, in *Pride and Prejudice*. Which, for all the popularity of that name now, it's not someone I'm really aspiring to be.

I remember reading the book and watching the movie when I was in high school and crying over Charlotte, who settled for the man everyone, including herself, couldn't stand.

Is that what I'm doing? Am I settling?

I don't feel like I'm settling. I wouldn't be thirty-one and single if I was settling. But I also feel like this goes back to my original question. What if I should be settling for the boat and instead I keep wanting more from God?

I rub my eyes and stare at my email. Ten from Joe. One from Joe's boss with my new client and her novel. A couple of spam emails and one from an address I don't recognize.

Hey Katie. This is J.T. from the other night. I hope you made it home safely. Just wanted to let you know that I had a great time and I hope I get to see you again next time you are in town. – J.T.

Well, that was a nice email.

Maybe there could be sparks there. I mean, it's not always love at first sight, right? Doesn't it sometimes have to develop and grow? Like the dad was telling Jennifer Lopez on *The Wedding Planner*?

I rake my hands back through my tangled hair and shake my head. This is ridiculous. I'm going to have to get out of the house if I have any hope of getting any work done today. I don't know why it is, but sometimes being away from my quiet home and in a restaurant with lots of people and noise makes me focus more. I've been like that since I was a kid in high school, though. I basically lived at one of the local coffee shops during finals week.

Seriously. I think they offered me a cot at one point.

I pull on a pair of jeans, a white T-shirt and a jacket and slip on a pair of shoes. I add a little bit of cover-up under my eyes and some mascara to try and mask some of the exhaustion and head out the door.

Panera is fairly quiet this morning and the good table by the fireplace is open. I set my laptop down, order myself a pumpkin spice latte and sit at the table, opening my computer and loading up all the emails from Joe.

Did you get the new assignment?

Katie? Good morning, sleepyhead!

See, I told you. You should have just stayed here one more night. Ten bucks says you're still in bed.

Though, if you had stayed here, you wouldn't be happy. We didn't get snow, but it's been raining nonstop since you left. The whole office smells like wet dog.

I look out the window at the overcast, but not raining, day and nod. I made the right decision.

I write Joe back and download my newest assignment. It's from a new author, Laura Yates. From the first glance, it looks like the same genre as Sue's book I just finished working on. Cozy mysteries are apparently on the comeback.

183

I write Laura a quick email introducing myself and letting her know the timeline. New authors are always anxious to know what is going on. I send the email, go get myself a refill of plain coffee and by the time I get back from adding sugar and cream, Laura has already written me back.

It's full of exclamation points and smiley faces and I just have this feeling this is going to be a rough book to edit.

Good grief. Maybe moving to Missouri landed me the short straw when it comes to my assignments from here on out.

"Switching up the days, huh?"

I look up and it's Luke Brantley. He's sitting down at the table next to me, setting a laptop down and pulling a Bluetooth headset off his ear, pocketing it.

I can't help the smile. "I was out of town on Monday," I say.

"Ah. Well, your table was very lonely when you were gone." He grins, adjusting his black glasses.

He really does have a very nice smile.

His hair looks crazier than normal today. Maybe the added humidity is making it curl more.

I bet he hates rainy weddings, considering he slicks his hair down when he sings.

"Did you have to go to New York?" he asks me.

I nod. "Two day meeting." I rub my cheek. "I got in about eleven-fifteen last night. Which is one-fifteen in New York. I'm having a hard time getting going this morning."

"I can imagine. Well, keep the refills coming, right?" He nods to my coffee cup.

I smile. "Exactly."

"So, Katie, I've been wanting to ask you, what are you up to this weekend? What do your evenings look like?"

I think I might be getting asked out on a date.

Two dates in a week. It's got to be a new world record in the life of Katie McCoy.

"Well, I have dinner with my grandmother every Friday night," I tell him. "It's our night together."

Luke smiles. "That's great. That's really great. I should establish some kind of regular weekly dinner with my grandparents. My grandfather isn't doing so well, lately. I'm going to see them on Friday night too, though. Okay, so how about Saturday night?"

"I don't think I have any plans," I say.

He grins. "Great! Would you like to get dinner with me? As much as I enjoy our working lunches, I think it would be nice to sit at the same table without our laptops and actually talk."

I smile and nervously tuck my hair behind my ears. "That would be nice."

"Six o'clock work for you?"

I nod. "Sure."

"Great! I can pick you up, if you'd like."

I still don't feel like I know Luke Brantley enough to give him my home address so I shake my head. "Oh, it's fine. I'll just meet you there." I try to say it super casually so he doesn't get his feelings hurt.

He smiles, a knowing expression on his face. "That works, too. Do you like Italian food?"

"Are there people out there who don't?"

"My thought exactly. Have you eaten at Pizoli's yet?"

I shake my head. "No." I think I heard Ashten mention it one time, though.

"Done. You'll love it. It's the best Italian food in the Midwest." He grins at me. "So. Six o'clock on Saturday at Pizoli's. It's the only one in town, so you can't miss it. And if you get lost, do you still have my card? My cell number is on there."

I nod. "Sounds great. And yeah, I still have your card."

"Perfect." He is still smiling, his brown eyes all crinkled up behind his glasses.

He's really a very nice looking guy. I smile back. There's this weird little tingle in my stomach and I can't tell if the pumpkin latte isn't sitting well, I'm nervous or I'm excited.

I leave a few minutes later just to spare myself from saying something dumb and making him take back his offer for dinner this weekend.

Luke grins at me. "See you on Saturday."

"See you Saturday," I nod. I climb into my car and take a deep breath.

Saturday.

CHAPTER *Fourteen*

I'm putting the vacuum back in the closet right as I hear the knock on the door. I open it and both Ashten and Eliza are standing there.

Eliza sniffs the air. "Hey!" she yells, accusingly. "You cleaned for us! I distinctly smell Pine-Sol."

"I thought it would be polite," I tell her, letting them in.

"The agreement was that we would never clean for each other. Remember? The whole point of this Bible study is to be real with each other and we can't do that if you are covering up your realness with Pine-Sol," she lectures, setting her Bible on my coffee table and taking off her coat.

"I put on deodorant this morning, so I guess I covered up that realness of me, too," I tell Eliza, who grins.

Ashten smiles at me. "Your house smells wonderful," she says.

"Thanks, Ashten." She still hasn't gotten back to me with a final answer about moving in here or not. Considering it's already November, I'm assuming her answer was no.

"You baked?" Eliza yells from the kitchen.

Ashten laughs. "Way to set the bar high, Katie."

"I just want you guys to feel comfortable here. Plus, I wanted cookies."

Eliza comes out of the kitchen eating a cookie and frowning at me.

"Are they not very good?" I'm immediately thinking through the ingredients I added to the batter.

"They're delicious," she says. "You just broke like every rule we created for this night, though."

"I thought cookies sounded good, so I made cookies. And it's been like a month since I vacuumed, so I vacuumed."

Eliza shakes her head. "Rule breaker."

"Sorry."

"I'm going to need more cookies before I'll be able to forgive you," she grins. "And probably the recipe."

"It's my Gram's recipe," I tell her, grabbing the plate of cookies from the kitchen and setting it on the coffee table. "I think you have to marry into the family to get the recipe."

"You don't happen to have any brothers, do you?"

"He's six."

"Cousins?"

"Sorry."

She sighs. "Guess we will just have to stay neighbors for the rest of our lives then. Speaking of which, Ashten, what's the deal on you moving here or not?"

Ashten nods to me. "Right. So sorry I haven't gotten back to you yet, Katie. Things have been nuts right now with progress reports. Anyway, I did talk to the management at the apartment and I guess my lease technically goes through the tenth, so if you're okay with me moving in then, I would love the room."

I grin. "That would be great!"

"But," she says, holding up a hand and interrupting my exclamation. "We are going to draw up an official lease and I am going to give you a fair rent. And I will share half of all of the utilities and half of the groceries."

"Fine by me," I say. "But you really don't have to pay for the utilities. Especially the cable and internet because I am already used to paying for those."

"So am I," Ashten says. "So you can just spend the extra on lattes or something."

"The way lattes are costing these days, you probably still won't be able to get more than one or two," Eliza says cheerfully. "Let's study the Bible."

There's another knock on my door right then and I look up. Eliza is here, Ashten is here.

Who else would be at my door?

"Oh," Eliza says, offhandedly. "I forgot to tell you, I invited a couple of other people, too. That's probably Mike. He's in town this week."

I thought I saw a blue truck outside Eliza's house earlier.

I open the door and Mike standing there. He looks grouchy, though I've never seen him look anything but grouchy, so maybe he just has one of those faces that always looks mad.

So weird that his sister is the outgoing, fun-loving, typically laughing Eliza.

"Hi Mike," I say, opening the door a little wider so I can let him inside.

"Katie, right?"

"That's right. Come on in. I've got cookies and I can make some coffee." I look at the girls. "Would anyone be up for a decaf?"

"I'm always good for coffee," Eliza says.

"Can I get a water?" Ashten asks and Eliza just shakes her head at Ashten.

Ashten grins.

"I'll take coffee, too," Mike says.

I close the door after Mike. "How many other people did you invite?" I ask Eliza before I start the coffee brewing. If more people are coming, I'm going to need to make a full pot.

"Like four or five people. Not too many. Mostly coworkers. Oh, and this random guy who I met in the hospital elevator."

I shake my head at Eliza. Apparently she has no problem giving out my home address to random strangers, even though I don't even give it out to someone I've seen and talked to several times at Panera.

"What?" Eliza asks.

"You gave out Katie's home address to a total stranger in the elevator?" Mike says, obviously frustrated. "See, this is what I'm talking about, Eliza! You have to be smarter and think safer. Remember what I've always told you? Where do you need to live?"

She sighs. "I need to live in the yellow."

"Yellow like liver failure?" Ashten asks.

"Yellow like caution," Mike says. "You need to always live in a cautionary state of mind. You need to constantly be thinking

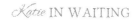

of what is the worst thing that could possibly happen right then and how would you handle it?"

Ashten looks at him. "So what's the worst thing that could happen right now?"

"Well, that random stranger could bust through the door with a weapon," Mike says.

"Thanks Mike. I'm sure I'll sleep great tonight, now," I say.

"That's why you guys all need to learn how to live in yellow," Mike says. "It's not supposed to be a scary thing, it's supposed to make you prepared and confident when something happens. I think you should all take a self-defense class."

"So, what would you do if someone came in here to rob Katie blind?" Ashten asks.

"I would attempt to get us all safely out another exit and then call the police," Mike says.

Eliza rubs her forehead. "Look, I'm sorry that I gave the other guy the address. He's not a total stranger, I've seen him around the hospital before. I think he's a resident in the OR. He's got a badge so I figured he was legit because you have to have a background check to work at the hospital."

"Unless he forged the badge," Mike says.

"Mike, life is not an *Ocean's Eleven* movie," Eliza tells her brother. "And if it is, I would like to know where George Clooney has been this whole time."

Mike shakes his head. "I'm just saying."

"I know, I know."

I go in the kitchen to make the pot of coffee and leave the siblings to their bickering while Ashten watches over them. I hear the front door open and close twice and when I get back into the room, there are two more girls and another guy, who I assume is the random stranger, sitting in my loving room, eating my cookies.

Eliza is certainly the social one.

I'm just thankful she offered to lead this week. I was definitely not planning on more than the three of us.

"Katie, these are a few of the people I work with. This is Kelly, Ashley and Liam."

"Hi guys," I say. I can see Mike eyeing Liam warily out of the corner of his eye. My fears are eased a bit when I see Liam. He's a petite guy with one of those nasty beards that isn't really tamed, it's just kind of growing haphazardly out of his face. And he's holding a Bible that looks semi-used.

So, that's good.

Unless it's borrowed.

Either way, he's probably a good inch or two shorter than me and likely doesn't weigh as much, so I think I could take him if he started getting ideas about my super expensive Corelle plates from the Target clearance section.

"Okay, so why don't we go ahead and start?" Eliza suggests. "We are reading in First John, guys."

I sit down on the couch in between Mike and Ashten. Eliza is sitting on the floor, straight-backed, legs crisscrossed, by the coffee table. The other three people have my other sofa.

We all open our Bibles and Eliza reads the first couple of verses.

"'What was from the beginning, what we have heard, what we have seen with our eyes, what we have looked at and touched with our hands, concerning the Word of Life— and the life was manifested, and we have seen and testify and proclaim to you the eternal life, which was with the Father and was manifested to us— what we have seen and heard we proclaim to you also, so that you too may have fellowship with us; and indeed our fellowship is with the Father, and with His Son Jesus Christ.'"

Eliza looks up. "So I did a little bit of research about what was going on during the time that John was writing this particular church. Apparently, some false teachers had gotten in and were teaching what was known as Gnosticism, or basically, that the body was sinful, the soul was not and since Jesus was perfect, He couldn't have come in bodily form."

I look up at Eliza. I'd studied the same few verses this week, but I didn't know the background. Suddenly, all the reiteration John was saying about seeing and hearing and knowing that Jesus had been here in the flesh made more sense.

"So, I guess I'll start off the discussion with a why. Why is it important for us that Jesus didn't just come as a spirit but that He came as a person with a physical body?"

It's a great question and one I'd never thought of before. And here I thought this study would be about love and that was basically it.

Already I can tell that this is going to be pretty great.

There's a verse that I can sort of half remember in the back of my mind, but I can't remember the reference. I'm pretty sure it's marked in my Bible though. I start flipping through the New Testament while I listen to what the others have to say.

"Wow, okay. That's a great question to start us out with, Eliza," Ashten says. "I think it's so important to know the background information of why these letters were written."

"Yep, I totally agree," Eliza says.

"And I think it's important that Jesus came in a body for a lot of reasons, the biggest being that if He didn't come physically, He couldn't have actually died for our sins."

Eliza is eating a cookie and she nods at Ashten. "Exactly. Great point."

"Or have done any of His miracles," one of the girls on the couch says. Kelly? I think her name was Kelly.

"Also right," Eliza says.

I finally find the verse and it's in the gospel of John. "Here, I was thinking about this verse," I say. "'And the Word became flesh, and dwelt among us, and we saw His glory, glory as of the only begotten from the Father, full of grace and truth.'"

"Right," Ashten says. "So it clearly says that Jesus was in the flesh and they could see His glory."

Eliza nods. "So John's defense against this false teaching was that he had seen Jesus, he had heard Jesus, he had touched Jesus and he was an eyewitness to His life. So what are some ways that we can defend our faith?"

We talk through that question and the other few that Eliza asks us for the next hour and a half. After listening to the others weigh in on their thoughts and hearing some of their testimonies, I get more and more thankful that Eliza invited these other people here. They add a lot to the discussion. Even Mike relaxes and talks.

Everyone leaves about nine o'clock, full of cookies, coffee and lots to think about.

I lock the door after everyone and smile as I carry the empty cookie plate back to the kitchen.

It was a great night.

Friday, I finish my initial read-through of the new book I'm working on around five o'clock. Perfect timing, since I'm supposed to be at Gram's in thirty minutes. She called me last night and asked if I could come at five-thirty and if baked potato soup and rolls sounded good for dinner.

I asked her if she knew me at all and she just started laughing. "Don't be late," she'd said as she hung up.

I close my computer, yawn as I stretch and go get a load of laundry started before I head out the door. I made sure I was in bed at nine o'clock last night, so I could do my normal morning routine today. I showered and got dressed this morning before work.

So much nicer to feel presentable. Even if I don't see anyone all day.

I drive to Gram's and get there at exactly five-thirty. She opens the door and shakes her head. "You're late."

"You told me five-thirty, Gram."

"When I was growing up, Mother told me that being on time was the same thing as being late."

"It's a new generation, Gram. On time is equal to early these days." I walk in her house and I can smell her infamous rolls. "Smells great, Gram!"

"Thanks, honey. Let me have your coat." She takes my jacket and hangs it on one of the hooks by the door.

I can hear people talking in the kitchen and I look at Gram. "Company again?" I ask her.

"Just some friends. Come in, come in."

We walk into the kitchen and I immediately see Luke Brantley standing by the stove, stirring the soup. Frieda and her husband – what was his name again? – are standing on the other side of the island. Frieda is lecturing Luke.

"I'm telling you, son. Mabel doesn't like people messing with her food."

"I'm not messing with it, Grandma. I'm just stirring it."

"She is telling the truth," Gram says, walking in the kitchen and shooing Luke away from the pot. "Luke, this is my granddaughter, K—"

"Katie," Luke says in surprise and then grins. "So you are Mrs. Laughlin's granddaughter." His grin widens. "I've heard a lot about you."

Frieda looks at us. "You two have already met?"

"Oh yeah, Grandma. We are old friends. Right, Katie?"

I nod to Frieda. "Nice to see you guys, again. We usually end up at Panera at that same time," I tell our confused grandmothers. Luke's grandpa doesn't seem to care that we already know each other.

I really wish someone would refer to him so I could remember his name.

Frieda nods. "Great. Then we can skip all the awkward parts of a first conversation. Katie, Lucas is my grandson."

I'm putting bits of conversations together from the last couple of weeks. "Wait, so at the wedding..." I say and Frieda nods.

"Yep. That was Lucas. He's a good singer, right? He's just too loud. I can't even get close enough to the stage to make a request or say hello to my own grandson. I keep telling him he needs to turn down the volume on the speakers. It's no wonder people are losing their hearing earlier and earlier. Why, I just heard a story last week about a man who lost his hearing at twenty-seven. They think it's because he was in a band." She looks at her grandson. "You'd better be careful, Lucas. You're a lot older than twenty-seven."

"Gram, I'm not a lot older than twenty-seven. Five years is not a lot older." He shakes his head. "And anyway, I don't really have a lot of say when it comes to the volume. Usually the venue controls it."

"Well, you should add volume control to your contracts with the venues. And five years is long enough for a baby to be born and go to school, Lucas," Frieda retorts. "That makes it a long time. Though, don't get me started on how early people are sending their kids to school these days. I passed a sign the other day where they were advertising preschool for two year-olds. Preschool! Why, at two years old, you could barely walk, Lucas."

"Mom says I started walking at nine months," Luke grins at his grandmother and I can see the little devilish glint in his eyes.

No wonder Frieda is such a spitfire if her family is all like this, too.

Gram waves her hands. "Now then, stop arguing, you'll deflate my rolls," she says, reaching for an oven mitt and pulling a huge Pyrex pan out of the oven that is crammed full of big, fluffy rolls.

"Mrs. Laughlin, those look amazing," Luke says.

I'm quietly trying to dab the drool off my chin.

Gram sets the pan on a cutting board on the counter and nods. "Thank you, Luke. Everyone get a bowl and we can eat in the dining room."

Frieda taps her husband's shoulder and nods to the bowl. "Time to eat," she says.

We all grab our bowls as we were told. Gram ladles the creamy soup with big hunks of potato into the bowls and we top them off with cheddar cheese, sour cream and fresh chives. Gram loads the hot rolls into a towel-lined basket and carries them into the dining room with her. She's already got the butter dish on the table.

Gram and I sit on one side of the table, Frieda and her husband take the other side and Luke gets the head of the table.

Unlike the last guest we had at the head of the table, though, Luke doesn't pull his phone out even once.

I can sense a set up again, but it honestly doesn't feel like one. Gram and Frieda argue back and forth and Luke interjects periodically. Frieda's husband just smiles and eats his soup and I would bet that his hearing aid isn't in again.

"So, Katie, how was New York?" Gram asks me, passing me another roll without me even asking.

Gram knows me too well. As amazing as this soup is, I could probably have just had a dinner of her rolls. I'm assuming that's why she gave me the smallest portion.

"It was good," I tell her. "Freezing cold."

"See? I told you. Did you take a coat like I told you?"

I nod. "Yes ma'am." Gram is probably The Weather Channel's only viewer, but she did warn me there was a cold snap coming through.

I guess the weather guys were right.

"You just never know when a freak snowstorm is going to hit these days," Gram says. "It's almost like we are living in that awful movie with the kids who had to burn the library books to live."

"What?" I ask.

"I don't remember the name of it, but there were wolves in it." Gram shakes her head. "Just a terrible movie."

"*Day After Tomorrow*," Luke supplies.

"Thank you. That was it," Gram says.

Luke nods. "Though I thought it wasn't getting as cold as it used to." Then he picks up his roll and dunks it in the soup.

Wrong. Just so wrong. You should never mar Gram's rolls with anything other than room temperature salted butter. That's it.

Gram shrugs. "We had lots of snow when I was a child as well. I remember we had such a bad snowstorm when I was about six that two kids died in it." She shakes her head. "Just terrible. They were walking home from school and got lost in the snow. Froze to death before someone found them."

"Oh my gosh," I say.

"It was awful," Gram nods and eats more soup.

This is totally Gram's generation, telling horrible stories about their childhood while they eat. I've had lunch with her a few times at the dining room of the senior complex that takes care of her house and it's amazing the stories you'll hear while you're attempting to eat. Especially if you get a seat by of the guys who served in the wars.

I still can't eat Frito pie.

"We still have some crazy weather every so often," Frieda says. "It's just not as normal, praise the good Lord. Remember that wedding you did a few years ago when we had snow in April?" She's looking at Luke, who just sighs.

"I think I'm still cold. I had to drink so much hot water to keep my throat from getting dried out from the cold that I had to go to the bathroom the whole reception. But, I had to hold it because we were in the middle of the set."

I grin.

"I do not understand this new trend of getting married outside," Frieda says. "You are supposed to be married in a church the way God intended."

Luke grins at his grandmother. "I don't seem to remember the reference for that Bible verse. Can you help me out with that?"

"And don't get me started on outdoor receptions," Frieda says, rolling her eyes and ignoring Luke. "Just a bad idea all around. What if it rains? What if it's windy or cold or we, God forbid, have a tornado? Anyway, the whole idea of a reception beyond some nuts and cake at your mother's house is just a ridiculous waste of money."

"Now, Frieda," Gram says. "I have been at some beautiful outdoor weddings. And you have to admit, you like going to the receptions and dancing."

Frieda smiles. "I do love to dance."

"As long as someone else can request the song. Right, Grandma?" Luke says.

"Exactly right, Lucas."

Luke takes a big drink of water and crunches a couple of cubes of ice in his teeth.

Even the sound makes a shiver run up my back.

I try not to think of it, but my mental copy of The Future Husband Wish List flashes in my brain.

No annoying eating habits.

Well, looks like Luke doesn't get a check mark by that one.

They leave about nine and Frieda claims she's already an hour past her bedtime as they walk out the door. Gram finally referred to Frieda's husband as Loren and I try to make a mental note.

I am so bad with names. It's one of the biggest side effects of working primarily on the computer – I can remember names when I see them written down, but I am terrible with them when I've only heard them. I'm one of those people who always advocates for name tags in meetings.

Basically, other people hate me.

Luke smiles at me as he leaves. "See you tomorrow night," he says in a quiet voice, so our grandmothers can't hear.

I smile. "See you then."

Gram closes the door behind them and looks at me. "So."

"So?"

"Much better than the Cell Phone Boy."

I laugh.

CHAPTER *Fifteen*

Saturday morning starts exactly how every Saturday morning should start. I don't even open my eyes until a little after nine o'clock and then I spend a good thirty minutes just slowly waking up.

I shuffle into the kitchen and get some coffee brewing before scrounging through the cabinets to see what I have to eat for breakfast. I haven't been grocery shopping in a bit and I'm all out of most of what the Boxcar children would have considered staples – bread, milk, cheese. I don't have any eggs, either.

See, this is why I need a chicken. Fresh, organic eggs every morning.

Of course, that also involves taking care of a chicken, so maybe I'll stick with the grocery store. Bird beaks kind of freak me out.

I find some stale Raisin Bran in the back of my pantry, pour a bowl and start eating it dry since I don't have any milk. The pathetic breakfast will have to do for today. I need to go to the store before I meet Luke tonight.

Maybe the Raisin Bran is bad. I get a little squirmy feeling in my stomach right then.

I get dressed, pull my hair back into a sloppy bun and swipe on some mascara. I'm planning on taking a shower before the date tonight, so there's no sense in getting dressed up now.

Especially just to go to the grocery store. I don't share the same ideals that *What Not To Wear* always touted. I'm pretty okay going to the grocery store in my yoga pants.

Though, granted, maybe I should listen more to Stacy and Clinton because don't people say the grocery store can be a great place for singles to meet? You know, the romance of two people spending way more money than they anticipated on toilet paper and pre-packaged meals?

I open my garage door and Eliza and Mike are hard at work on her front yard. She waves me over and I slide my sunglasses on to cover up the lack of any real makeup on my face. Now I'm wishing I had at least put on real pants. And left my UGG boots in the closet. Somehow it went from being fairly crisp outside to unseasonably warmish today.

"Hey," I say, walking over.

"Good morning!" Eliza says, all chipper. "How are you this morning?"

"Hungry. I'm going to the grocery store."

She tsks at me. "You're breaking my mother's first cardinal rule of adulthood. Don't go grocery shopping on an empty stomach."

Mike looks over at me as he tills up the flower bed in Eliza's front yard. "Morning, Katie."

"Hey, Mike."

"I made blueberry muffins this morning. Go get one."

"I'm not going to take one of your muffins, Eliza."

"Yes, you are. Please. I insist. I have to work tomorrow, which means I'll just grab a Clif bar on my way out the door.

Mike doesn't need the extra carbs anyway. His metabolism is starting to slow down."

"Gee, thanks," Mike says, rolling his eyes and taking his backward baseball cap off long enough to swipe his forearm across his forehead. "Remind me why I drove all the way down here to help you out this weekend?"

"I don't think I asked for help," Eliza grins at him. "You miss your sister. Just admit it."

Mike looks at her and shakes his head. "Anyway, Katie, please help yourself to the muffins. Eliza made three dozen of them for the two of us."

"I'm still used to football player Mike's appetite," Eliza says, grinning.

"Because that was so recent," Mike says. "My last game was what? Over ten years ago?"

"Did you play college football?" I ask Mike.

"For a couple of years," Mike says. "I wasn't that great, but it did pay for school, so that was nice."

"So, basically, he was good, but not that good. He didn't get to go to the NFL," Eliza says.

"Thanks."

"No problem. Please go get a muffin, Katie. And if you want to put off the store, you're welcome to help us out here."

"What are you doing?" I ask.

"Well, I think part of the reason those flowers that were in here when I moved in had such a hard time growing was because of the slant of this flower bed. So, we're going to raise it up a few inches in the back and Mike's going to add some sprinklers. That way, it can be on a timer and I don't have to remember to water them." She grins at me. "Sort of like that auto bill pay feature my bank offers that I love."

Mike sighs. "Eliza..."

"I know, I know. You hate the auto bill pay."

"You need to be reviewing the bills before they just suck however much money they want out of your account. What if they make a mistake and you end up paying some ridiculous amount? What if you aren't able to get it back?"

I smile. I barely know him, but Mike seems like he can be so glass half-empty. Especially compared to Eliza.

I go inside and there is a Tupperware container filled with blueberry muffins on Eliza's counter, alongside two coffee mugs with a few tablespoons of cold coffee in each one.

I guess they were pretty anxious to get outside if they can't even finish their coffee. I grab a muffin and head back outside while I take a bite.

Oh my goodness. These muffins are amazing.

"Good night, Eliza, these are incredible," I tell her.

She grins at me, swiping a stray hair that had slipped out of her French braid back behind her ear. "Thanks!" she says. "It's an old family recipe."

"Those are the best kind."

"I wouldn't know. We don't have any old family recipes," Eliza says.

"But you just said—"

"It's an old family recipe, but it's not my family's old recipe," she says. "I found it on Pinterest. It was that blogger's great-grandmother's recipe. Or something like that. Though, between you and me, I kind of doubt that cake flour has been around that long."

Mike looks at me, squinting in the sunlight. "She's just a joy to talk to, isn't she?"

I laugh. "Oh, Eliza."

"Now. Are you up for installing sprinklers?" she asks me.

"I really need to go grocery shopping," I tell her.

"Good. Get out while you can," Mike says.

"Way to chase off the help, Michael," Eliza says. "We could have been done in a couple of hours."

"Katie, have you ever installed a sprinkler drip system before?" Mike asks me.

"Can't say that I have."

"Eliza, she wouldn't have made anything go any faster. Enjoy the grocery store, Katie. Go. Run. Hurry, before she keeps stalling you," Mike says and he smiles at me.

I don't think I've ever seen him smile but something pretty great happens to his face when he does. His eyes sort of get all squinchy, which makes his eyelashes look crazy long and thick and he gets these laugh lines by his mouth. Apparently, the man does know how to smile and does it more frequently than he lets on.

It's kind of hard to look away.

I smile back at him and finally look over at Eliza. "Need anything?" I ask her.

"A slushy would be great."

"It's barely ten in the morning," I tell her.

"So?"

"So, I thought there was some rule against slushies before the afternoon. Isn't that why Sonic's slushy happy hour is in the afternoon?"

Eliza shrugs. "It's hot."

"It is pretty warm today," I nod.

"You probably should have left the boots at home," Eliza says.

"Well, I didn't know it was this warm when I got dressed this morning," I tell her. "My house got cold last night." I remember waking up because my shoulder and arm were cold. "So, this is kind of weird."

"Fall is always weird. So, would you plant the tulip bulbs now or would you wait?" Eliza asks. "I just don't want them to start growing too early and get killed by the frost."

"Honestly, Eliza, my experience with bulbs is pretty much narrowed to the electrical kind," I tell her.

Mike grins. Again. I look over at him and then pull my gaze back over to Eliza.

She is smirking and I can feel my cheeks starting to flush. And it has nothing to do with the warmer temperatures.

"I'm going to go get a glass of water," Eliza says. "I'll be right back." She leaves and it's just me and Mike.

He watches her go and then turns to me. "Hey, thanks for making her feel so welcome here," he tells me.

"Of course. She's really fun to be around," I say.

He nods. "She is. Hey," he says, pausing and looking down at the dirt under his feet. He squints up at the sun and then looks at me. "Hey," he says again. "I don't know if you…I was thinking maybe we could potentially go get coffee sometime?"

Based on the way he is asking and nervously picking at his work gloves, I'm assuming this coffee wouldn't include his sister.

I can feel my cheeks heating up even more.

"Um, sure," I say. "That would be fun."

"Great!" he says. "I'll give you a call. I think I'll be back in a couple of weekends, so maybe then?"

"Um, yeah. That should work," I nod, feeling like I'm back in junior high or something.

Eliza comes back out and hands Mike a plastic cup the size of a bucket. It's full of ice water.

"Thanks," he tells her.

"Sure, no problem." She looks at me and I know she sees the neon shade my cheeks are currently sporting. "What did I miss?"

Time to go.

"All right, well, have fun getting the sprinklers all hooked up," I say and hightail it back across the street. I briefly consider changing my shoes and then just decide to leave.

What is going on? I already have a date tonight with Luke. And I had a date earlier this week with J.T.

And now, I apparently have a coffee date with Mike in the next couple of weekends.

I start my car and rub my forehead.

Thirty-one years with basically no prospects and now, there are three sweet, seemingly normal Christian men around me.

Is this the definition of "when it rains, it pours"?

Mike and Eliza are gone when I get back and big part of me is relieved. I unload my groceries and decide that today is going to be a day to clean up around the house. I clean the toilets, vacuum the carpets and reorganize my closet so it will hold the boxes from the guest room.

Ashten is planning on moving in next weekend. She sent me a text while I was at the store asking for me to come up with a lease she can sign.

Aside from just writing on a post-it note, "hey, why don't you live here?", I'm not sure what she wants from me. I google a few things when I finish cleaning, but everything looks too formal for just two friends living together.

I mean, honestly, she's helping me out way more than I'm helping her. Even a few hundred dollars a month in rent from her is still a few hundred dollars I can put into my savings. I actually have a pretty good amount in there already.

Maybe I'll take myself to Disney in a few months.

Doesn't that sound fun? Disney by myself.

I get in the shower and step out a few minutes later, wringing the water from my hair. My hair is way too long. I squeeze my hair from my scalp down to the ends and there's enough water pooling on the shower floor to water a small vegetable garden for a few days.

Maybe I should start recycling that water.

I imagine what all that would entail.

Or not.

I hope I'm not the only person who has crazy thought trains in the shower.

I get a comb through my hair, add in mousse and leave in conditioner and I blow dry it upside down so it has a little bit of volume to it. I don't often straighten it or use a curling iron on it since it has so much natural wave anyway, but tonight is a special occasion, so I take my time.

It takes me almost forty-five minutes just to do my hair, and I remember why I usually just let it do it's own thing. This is ridiculous. If I'm going to start actually styling it, I need to cut it quite a bit shorter.

I put on my makeup and I'm ready to leave by twenty minutes until six o'clock. Pizoli's is about fifteen minutes away and I'd rather get there a few minutes early so I can look at the menu. I tried to look it up today online and they didn't have it on there.

Every restaurant should always put their menus online. I'm one of those people who likes to know what I'm ordering before I even get in the car to leave. It used to make my mom insane. She was more of a figure it out when you get there type of person, but then it would take her twenty minutes to look over the menu. Meanwhile, I'd be starving for whatever I was already planning on eating.

I find the restaurant without a problem. It's decorated super nice inside. There's a huge fountain in the waiting area, surrounded by lots of Tuscan colors and flowers. Italian music plays in the background.

There are about twenty people crammed in here and the restaurant looks packed.

"Can I help you?" a hostess in front of me asks from behind an old wooden desk.

"Hi, yeah, do you guys take reservations?" No sense in me putting my name on the list if Luke already has a reservation.

"No, ma'am, we don't."

"Okay. How long is the wait?" Based on the expressions I'm seeing around me, it looks like most people have already been here a long time.

If there's one thing that Carrington Springs people like to do, it's eat out.

"About an hour to an hour and a half," the girl tells me and I balk.

"Holy cow."

"Yeah, weekends are a little crowded. Can I put your name on the list?"

"I mean, I guess so. It's Katie."

"We'll call you in a little bit," she says, giving me a blinking buzzer. She looks at the people behind me. A line has formed while I've been talking to her.

"Can I help you?"

I take my buzzer and go stand by the fountain since there is no where to sit.

"Hey, Katie."

Luke is here and he's looking around the packed restaurant with wide eyes. "Wow, it looks like we weren't the only ones with this idea," he says.

"It's an hour to an hour and a half wait," I tell him, holding up the buzzer.

He whistles.

"Yep."

"Okay, then. Well. Want to stay here? Or does someplace else sound good to you?" He smiles at me. "You look beautiful, by the way."

I am blushing.

He looks pretty good himself. He's combed his hair back like he does for weddings and he's wearing a white button down shirt and jeans. He's looking around at all the discontented, hungry people and then he shakes his head.

"What about that steak place off the interstate?" he asks me. "Ruby's?"

I shrug. "Anyplace might be this crowded, but that sounds good, too." I haven't scoped out the menu yet, but I can probably do that after I drive over.

"I'll call them real quick." He pulls his cell phone out of his pocket and googles the number. "I'll be right back." He steps out of the restaurant where it's a little quieter to call.

I look around at the people, trying not to make eye contact with anyone because it's just one of those awkward things, like looking at people riding with you on an elevator. I'm not sure why.

Luke comes back in a minute later. "It's only a fifteen minute wait over there and they have a call ahead list, so I put our name on it."

"Sounds good."

I give the hostess the buzzer back and we walk out into the finally cooling off day.

"This weather has just been weird today," I say to him. Now I'm almost wishing I'd brought a jacket. I decided on skinny jeans and a long tunic-style top and ballet flats. Cute, but not warm. If it's already getting chilly, I'm going to be freezing by the end of the evening.

"Fall here is usually pretty inconsistent. Want to just ride with me?" Luke asks as we walk to the parking lot. "We can come back and pick up your car after dinner."

"Sure," I nod. "Thanks, that sounds great."

He leads me over to a dark green Toyota 4Runner and opens the passenger door for me.

"Thanks," I say again, climbing inside.

It's always a good view into someone's life when you are looking around their car. My dad was fastidious about our cars when I was growing up. He cleaned them out every night when he got home from work and vacuumed them every Saturday morning. I used to wake up to the sound of the little vacuum he kept in the garage specifically for the cars. It made me nuts sometimes, but it was really nice always driving a clean car. I'm pretty much a neat freak about my car, though I don't vacuum it every single weekend.

It does not seem that Luke is that type of guy.

The passenger seat is clean, but there is stuff everywhere else. There are piles of papers in the backseat, jackets, empty water bottles and who knows what else back there. I can't even see the floorboard.

I think my heart is palpitating.

Luke climbs in and looks at the car. "The joy of working for yourself is that your car becomes your office," he says. "Sorry for the disaster."

"It's fine," I say, because that's just what you say when someone says something like that. Though honestly, I'm remembering some of the online stories I've read where they find living animals in people's cars because they are so incredibly disgusting.

I try to calm my train of thought because it's not helping the heart rate. It's not that bad, I guess. It's mostly papers. And I don't see or smell any food containers, which I guess was the biggest reason for those people finding things living in their cars. They would get leftovers from a restaurant and then forget to take them out of the car.

Why go through the trouble of boxing up leftovers if you are just going to leave them to get all smelly and moldy in your car?

Luke starts driving to Ruby's, which is about five or so minutes down the street. "Sorry for the change in venue," he says.

"Spoken like a true wedding singer," I tell him.

He grins. "Sometimes it comes out."

"Do you like singing at weddings?" The only thing that comes to my mind when I think of wedding singers is Adam Sandler.

Luke smiles at me. "I love it," he says, and you can just tell he really does. "It's so much fun to have such a unique part of what is hopefully that couple's most wonderful day of their lives. There's a lot of pressure too, because you'll notice that you rarely remember the wedding band if they are good, but you definitely remember them if they are bad."

"How does it work with your band?" I ask. "Did you find them?"

He nods. "We all met in college and started messing around with different instruments and vocals in Sam's dorm room. Next thing we knew, one of the guys down the hall had just gotten engaged and his fiancée was walking past as we were playing one day. She marched right in, saw us all standing there and booked us for the wedding." He grins. "I think she was just shocked that we weren't listening to a CD or something. It was a big lift to our band's self esteem."

"How come your cards only say your name and not the band's name, too?"

"After college, a few of the guys took off for different jobs around the country, and so I have a pick-up band who works with me. I have about four guys I know who play each instrument and depending on availability, it can change. It was easier for me to be the front runner and take charge of everything. I make it worth their time to come, so I've never been short someone." He grins at me. "Can you play the trumpet? You can ask around, I pay very generously."

I shake my head, clutching my purse tightly on my lap so it doesn't get lost in the pile of papers at my feet. "Sorry. You're looking at someone who has exactly zero musical capabilities whatsoever."

"Come on. Everyone can sing."

"You have obviously never sat next to met in church," I tell him.

"I would if you'd come visit tomorrow," he grins over at me, pulling into the Ruby's parking lot.

I nod. I'd actually talked to Eliza and Ashten about it and they were both up for trying somewhere new. "It's not like we're super involved here," Eliza had said.

"I think we're going to come tomorrow," I say to Luke. "What service do you go to?"

"The ten-thirty."

And yet another way that Luke is totally different from my dad. When I was growing up, we were always – rain or shine – at the earliest church service. Mostly so that Dad could have time to go back home and catch whatever football game was on TV at eleven. Whatever the reason, I ended up sticking with it when I grew up and moved out.

There's something about getting up and heading out that just feels like a Sunday morning.

The church I went to in college used to serve breakfast before the early service, so that was an even bigger reason to go for a broke college student. There was a lady who would come make breakfast who had hands down the best pancakes in the city. Sometimes, she would even add this homemade pecan streusel to the top of them.

I'm pretty sure there were hallelujahs whispered over the breakfast on those mornings.

"I usually sit on the right side of the auditorium," Luke says as he parks.

I nod. "I'll look for you tomorrow, then."

"Sounds great. I think you'll really enjoy it!"

We get out of the car and he holds the door to the restaurant for me. Ruby's is built on a hill, so we climb the staircase to get up to the actual restaurant and walk into the waiting area. The Italian place must have been running some kind of special, because this place is basically empty compared to Pizoli's.

I don't know why, but it always makes me nervous going to an empty restaurant. Did they get a bad report? Did someone die of salmonella or listeria or scurvy or one of those awful things after eating here?

"This is much better," Luke says, walking in.

I guess the thought of death by steak doesn't enter his mind. Though, I think bacteria is killed by heat, so maybe if I just get my steak cooked well done tonight, I'll be okay.

I am ridiculous.

Luke goes over to the hostess stand and we are sitting at a table for two near the windows overlooking the town a few minutes later.

"This is nice," Luke says, looking out at the city lights starting to come on.

"It is," I nod. There's a lantern with a lit candle inside on our table and the whole restaurant is on the dimmer side.

It feels romantic.

I look over at Luke as he studies the menu. I guess he's wearing contacts because his glasses are a no-show tonight. He's got just the slightest dark stubble across his chin and it actually looks really nice.

He's a nice guy, he's a Christian, he can sing. I mean, there's three of the things on my list right there.

Though, if his car is any indication, he's not a very neat and tidy person. And way back when, that was a big thing on my list, too. I'm not down with the whole coming home and dumping everything on the couch or floor.

"What are you going to get?" Luke asks, and I realize I haven't even looked at the menu yet.

"Oh, um, I'm not sure," I say, opening it and pretending that I've been studying it for the last five minutes. It takes a few seconds for my eyes to even be able to make out the wording. It's pretty dimly lit in here and the font is tiny.

You'd think they would compensate for the poorly lit room with bigger print. Or if they wanted to do a tiny print, they could up the lighting a little bit.

Finally, I can read the words. There's all different cuts of steaks, some roast plates, a few chicken plates and a fish and chips plate that looks pretty delicious.

I'm a sucker for fried fish.

Um. No pun intended.

"I think I'm going to get the fish and chips," I tell Luke. Plus, it's right in the middle as far as prices go.

I never know how to do this when it comes to a date. If I order too cheap, I'm worried they'll think I don't think they can actually afford to take me out, but if I order too expensive, I worry that they'll think I'm a spoiled snob.

So, I always try to find the cheapest entree and the most expensive entree and go somewhere in the middle.

At Serendipity's the other night, it was a lot harder, because they are the ones known for their one thousand dollar sundae.

Yes. One *thousand* dollars. Apparently, there are actual fourteen carat gold flecks in the sundae.

I'm not sure why you would want to eat metal, but I guess some people do. I can't imagine what it would do to your digestion.

I think I might be hanging out with my grandmother too much if I'm actually concerned about digestive issues right now.

"The fish and chips looks great," Luke says. "I'm going with the filet and the mashed potatoes."

"Steak and potatoes guy, hmm?" I ask him.

"Yep. Well, sometimes. I don't grill very often just for myself. I grill when my mom or my grandparents come over, though. And I'll usually order a steak if I go out. But I don't go out to places that serve steak very often."

"So your mom still lives here?" I ask, trying to open up the conversation even though I already know the answer.

He nods. "I'm sure you'll probably meet her at some point. She was working the other night or she would have been at your grandmother's. By the way, I have spent the last three years hearing all about Mabel Laughlin's beautiful, single granddaughter and how we were going to have to meet someday." He grins across the table at me, his eyes glowing in the candlelight. "I'm glad to see my grandmother was right this time."

All of a sudden, I'm incredibly thankful for the dim lighting. Especially when he picks up the water glass the waiter leaves and spends the next couple of minutes crunching the ice.

CHAPTER *Sixteen*

Nine o'clock and I am up, showered, dressed and sitting on my couch with a cup of coffee, looking at the clock.

This is just weird to still be home on a Sunday. For all the times that I have wanted to sleep in and skip church, I could never do it. Not if this is what it feels like.

And I'm not even skipping church. I'm just going later.

So weird.

I open my computer on the sofa cushion next to me and bring up my email inbox. None from Joe, thankfully. I'm not going to be working today.

There is one from J.T. though.

Hey Katie,

Just seeing if you have another trip to the city scheduled yet. How is the editing going? It has been incredibly cold here but they are saying it's just a snap and we should have some warmer weather again before it gets cold for good.

Just wanted to say hi. Hope you are doing well. Enjoy your weekend!

-J.T.

I look at the email and lean back against the couch.

J.T. Mike. Luke.

Three different men in every sense of the word.

J.T. is all business-like and classic New York, even down to his haircut. He's totally the type of guy who wouldn't even question raising kids in the city and living his entire life in an extremely overpriced apartment high above 5th Avenue.

Mike is the world's biggest worrywart, I'm pretty sure. I've never seen a brother more concerned over his sister. Though, hearing their background has made me a little more understanding of it. And knowing Eliza makes me even more understanding – the girl is adorable and hilarious, but she does make me worried sometimes, too. You can tell, though, that Mike is a really hard worker, especially when it comes to things he needs to do for his sister.

And then, there's Luke. Luke, who seems perfect, but who keeps having these weird quirks that make me a little nuts.

I rub my forehead. I've never experienced anything like this before. I'm not the girl who's always had all kinds of boyfriends or dates. I didn't even get asked out until I was twenty-four years old.

By then, I had already been in six of my friends' weddings.

It was frustrating, to say the least.

Then, I hit the stage where people kept asking if I was dating someone or not and kept offering to set me up on blind dates. I took them up on their offers twice and when both of those fizzled out before they even started, it was just easier to do my own thing and be quietly resentful every time someone announced their engagement or pregnancy. Everyone around me was moving on with life, and I was stuck on this hamster wheel.

I close my eyes and lean my head back on the sofa.

"All I ever wanted You to give me was a husband, Lord," I say quietly into the empty apartment.

Now there are three potential possibilities.

So why do I feel like this?

Eliza rides with me over to Luke's church.

"So what is the name of this church again?" she asks me, flipping the sun visor down and using the mirror to put on mascara.

"Cross Point," I tell her. "Are you seriously still getting ready? I've been ready for over an hour."

"Dude, you need to learn the art of sleeping in," Eliza says, brushing the wand over her lashes. "I slept until nine forty-five."

I shake my head. It's ten-fifteen right now. "Don't you ever wake up and feel like you've wasted the day away? How in the world do you get ready that quickly?"

She sighs. "I have failed in my neighborly duties."

I grin. "What do you mean?"

"I mean, I haven't taught you the correct way to enjoy your weekend. You need to learn to just let the world go on. There is no wasteful moment that is spent asleep in a nice, soft bed. And I learned the art of the quick shower in nursing school. It's a life skill that has proven pretty much invaluable."

"My dad would have totally disagreed with you."

"With the quick shower?"

"With the sleeping the day away."

"Eliza's words of wisdom right there," she says, screwing the wand back into the mascara bottle and pushing the visor back up. "So."

"So?"

"I noticed you and Mike looked like you both had gotten a little sun when I came back out the other day. And I'm just here as a medical professional to tell you that you can't get that pink from the sun so quickly." She grins at me. "Might there be some attraction between you and my brother?"

I shake my head. "Busy body."

"Such a Jane Austen comment. He's my brother and you're my neighbor and dear friend, so I'm allowed to be busy when it comes to you guys."

"Oh, really?"

"Really. It's in a handbook somewhere, I'm sure." She grins over at me. "So, did he ask you out?"

I hate that I can feel my cheeks pinking even as I try to roll my eyes. "Eliza, it's not a big deal, I promise."

"He totally asked you out." She is jumping in the passenger seat, squealing. "Oh, Katie, I am *so* excited! We will be sisters!"

"Okay, whoa. Hold on there, missy."

"We could spend every holiday together!" She grabs my arm at a stoplight and looks very seriously in my eyes. "And Katie, you have no idea how much fun I am to be around during the holidays."

Oh, I didn't doubt it.

"Eliza," I say, attempting to calm her down. "First off, we aren't getting married, it was just a potential coffee date."

"You've got to start somewhere."

I ignore her point and turn into the church's parking lot.

"What's the second off?"

"What?"

"You had a first off. What's the second one?"

I park and huff my breath out, gripping the steering wheel and turning off the ignition. "Eliza," I say slowly again, and I can't figure out how to put into words what I'm thinking. "Never mind. Let's go on in. I bet Ashten is already here."

"We'll finish this talk another time, okay?" Eliza asks, climbing out of the car.

"Oh, yay."

I grab my Bible and my purse and feel my phone buzz as we walk across the parking lot. It's a text from Ashten.

Two mins away. At the light.

I gesture to Eliza and we step aside to wait out front for Ashten. Her car pulls into the parking lot a couple of minutes later and she hurries out, slinging her purse over her shoulder.

"Sorry, sorry," she says, all out of breath when she catches up to us. "I got caught up packing." She shakes her head. "This late service thing is really throwing me for a loop today."

"You and me both," I tell her.

Eliza just sighs. "I mean, it's like I've completely failed as your friend," she tells us as we walk inside.

The foyer area is small, but cute and well laid out. There's a long bar with a few different coffeepots on it on the right and on the left are the doors to the sanctuary. There isn't a whole visitor welcome crew, but we do get a couple of friendly smiles from the ladies handing out the programs.

I haven't mentioned Luke to either of the girls yet. Mostly because I'm not sure what to say about him. "Hey, girls, this is a random guy I met at Panera"?

It just sounds a little sketchy.

Maybe it is a little sketchy.

So, I just kept my mouth closed. When they'd asked why the late service time, I'd kind of ignored the question.

We find some seats on the aisle towards the right of the church, even though Eliza kept wanting to go sit in front.

"Why do you like the front so much?" Ashten asks her as Eliza grumpily sits down next to us in the middle.

"I don't know. When I was really little, my parents made us sit in the front row so I would pay attention and wouldn't be all squirmy through the whole sermon."

"Why did sitting in front help?" I ask. "Wouldn't that make it worse?"

"Are you kidding? Our preacher was known for getting all animated. The front row was the splash zone, my friend. I had to pay attention to know when to duck and cover."

Ashten laughs. "You are disgusting."

Eliza grins. "I speak the truth. I never showered on Sundays until after we got back home."

"You are gross," Ashten grins.

"Hi there."

I look up and Luke is standing in the aisle by our row, holding a Styrofoam cup with steaming black liquid in it. He's back to sporting his curly hair and glasses and he's wearing slim-cut jeans and a long-sleeve flannel shirt.

"Hi," I say, smiling.

Ashten and Eliza both just look at me.

"Hi," Eliza says, standing and sticking her hand out to Luke. "I'm Eliza. This is Ashten. And I take it you already know Katie."

"This is Luke Brantley," I tell them both.

Ashten is squinting her eyes at him and I know she's trying to place where she knows him from. I wonder how often Luke gets that look from people.

He smiles at her and hands her a business card. "Nice to meet you both," he says.

Ashten looks at the picture on the card and snaps her finger. "Oh! That's where I know you!"

Apparently, fairly often if he knows they are going to need to see him all spiffed up to place him.

He grins. "Can I sit with you guys?"

"Sure," Eliza says, and immediately shoves Ashten's shoulder so that Luke is on the aisle and sitting next to me.

Nothing like being good and awkward about it.

"What do you do, Luke?" she asks.

"I'm a consultant," he tells her.

"And he also sings at weddings," Ashten says. "You just sang at my friend's wedding last month. It was great. Best wedding music I've heard in a long time."

"Thanks, I appreciate that," Luke says, smiling at her.

"So, wait, you're a singer?" Eliza asks.

He nods. "Mostly on the weekends."

"That's so cool. I always wanted to be a singer, I just wasn't given the gift of a good voice. I was that kid who always tried out for the lead in the church Christmas musicals, but always got cast as Angel Number Six."

Luke grins. "Well, but think about how lonely the angelic choir would have sounded without that sixth voice," he says.

"Now you sound like my mother."

"So do you like listening to Sinatra too, or just singing it?" Ashten asks him.

Luke shrugs. "I like listening to it. I honestly like listening to almost everything except metal."

A band appears on stage and a man wearing a Polo shirt and jeans picks up a guitar and leans into the microphone. "Why don't we all stand and sing?" he asks, and the congregation quiets their chatter as everyone stands up.

We sing three songs and it's nice. It's not crazy outgoing like First Community, but you can tell that the people on the stage aren't there for a performance, they are there to worship. We sing a mix of hymns set to modern music and praise songs like I hear on the radio. The vocals aren't as polished as First Community, but they also aren't bad.

I'm totally self-conscious singing next to Luke. He sings with his eyes closed, one hand holding his coffee, the other hand raised. His voice is amazing. It's like I'm standing next to a curlier, younger Michael Buble in church.

I'm like Eliza. I was never cast as the Christmas choir musical lead, either. Actually, I never even tried out because I was so terrified that I might fail at it.

My dad always said that "failure" was not in the McCoy dictionary.

Better to not be the McCoy who put it in there, then.

I sing quietly.

We sit down a few minutes later and a blond man who is probably in his late forties stands at the podium and adjusts his notes. "Let's pray first," he says, and prays a simple prayer that is both heartfelt and not flashy.

He preaches for forty minutes on the last part of Hebrews chapter four. "God gave us these words because He knows us, He knows our hearts. He knows that we struggle with guilt, with temptation, with complaining, with discontentment. And yet, where are we supposed to go with these feelings?" He looks around the congregation. "Are we supposed to stuff them down, pretend they don't exist? Have you ever begged and pleaded with God for something and He hasn't given it to you?"

It takes everything in me not to fidget under the pastor's gaze. He's talking to me. I know he's talking to me.

"Look at this verse with me once more. 'Let us draw near with confidence to the throne of grace, so that we may receive mercy and find grace to help in time of need.'" He looks up from his Bible. "God doesn't call us to run away from Him in a time of need. He doesn't call us to stuff our feelings down or put on a happy face. It says nothing in here about acting like everything's

fine and not acknowledging when something isn't going the way we had planned."

Eliza and Ashten are writing notes like crazy on their bulletins. I don't move for fear of missing even one word that the pastor is saying. There will be time to write it down later.

Right now, my soul just needs to listen.

"Friend," the pastor says, looking warmly at the people. "God sits on a throne of *grace*. We can draw near to that throne with confidence, knowing that He has made us, He knows us and He has plans for our lives that go so far beyond what we could have ever imagined for ourselves. He longs to give us mercy. He loves to give us grace. And He meets us in our time of need. Let's pray."

He prays, we sing two more songs and the congregation erupts into the chatter they had set aside for the service.

Eliza, Ashten and Luke are immediately talking about the sermon, about the singing, about Luke and his consulting jobs and how we met.

I listen to their conversation and interject occasionally, but I'm having trouble focusing.

I can feel the nudge in my spirit and I don't know what I need to do.

CHAPTER *Seventeen*

"Let's go get lunch," Luke says as we walk out of the church. I think he's talking to all three of us, so I look at the other girls and they both shrug and nod.

"Sure," Ashten says. "I can pause with the packing."

"I'm going to see what Mike is up to. Maybe he can join us," Eliza says.

"He didn't want to come to church?" Ashten asks.

Eliza shakes her head. "He was going to come. Right as we were walking out the door, my alarm started beeping with all these errors and he had to stay back and fix it since he's leaving right after lunch to go back to St. Louis. I was in the way, I think, so he made me come."

I had actually wondered why Mike hadn't come, too.

"I'll see if he's fixed it." She pulls out her phone.

"What sounds good for lunch?" Luke asks me.

I shrug. "Actually, I think a cheeseburger sounds really good."

"Oo! And a milkshake," Eliza says.

"And sweet potato fries," Ashten adds.

Luke grins. "You guys are easy. Have you guys been to Farmer's yet?"

Eliza and I shake our heads and Ashten nods. "It's really good," she tells us. "Best sweet potato fries in the county. And I can only say that because my family doesn't serve sweet potato fries."

Luke looks at her. "You guys in the restaurant business?"

"Minnie's Diner."

"No way! I've been eating there since I was old enough to chew my own food," Luke says.

Ashten grins. "Hey, me too."

He laughs. "That's cool. So, no sweet potato fries there, huh? You guys do have good burgers, though."

"Thanks. My grandpa is pretty proud of them."

"We could go there, too," Eliza says. "Unless you are really wanting the fries, Ashten."

Ashten thinks on it. "Actually, let's go to Minnie's. Have you ever eaten there, Katie?"

I shake my head. "Nope."

Eliza's phone buzzes. "Mike just finished reprogramming my alarm. Don't tell him this, but I think it's because I accidentally tripped the fuse when I was trying to use my bread machine while vacuuming and running the dryer."

I grin. "I'll try my best to avoid telling him that."

"And he's good with burgers."

"Minnie's, it is," Luke nods. "Does everyone know where it is?"

I don't, but Eliza is nodding her head and she rode with me, so I figure she can lead me to it. Plus, I can also just follow Ashten.

Minnie's Diner is a couple of minutes outside town. There's a huge, huge parking lot. It's already almost full and there are three buses parked along the back of the lot. The restaurant itself is gigantic, huge and sprawling. I don't know that I would necessarily classify this place as a "diner".

When I think of diner, I think of somewhere that Guy Fieri would visit where he barely fits in the kitchen with his spiked up hair.

"Good night, this place is ginormous," I say to Eliza when we park.

"Wait until you see the inside."

We climb out and Ashten leads the way inside, bypassing the line and waving at us to hang out in the lobby. Luke strolls in then, pocketing his keys and looking at the crowd around us.

"I take it we are not the only people who had this idea," he says.

"What?" Eliza yells at him.

"It's busy!" he shouts back.

A couple of minutes later, Ashten reappears and grabs a couple of menus from the hostess stand. "Come on, guys," she says, and we get to skip ahead of the crowd.

I guess there are perks to being the granddaughter of the owners.

Mike comes in right as we are walking back and Ashten leads us through a couple of packed rooms, down two hallways and finally to a large room with windows that overlook this huge grassy field. She nods to a large booth, "Can we all fit in there?"

We slide in and there is room to spare. She sets the menus down and then sits as well.

"So, what is good here?" I ask.

"Everything," Luke and Ashten say together.

Ashten grins. "My grandmother's favorite is her fried frog legs, but I wouldn't necessarily recommend those if you have any sort of a sensitive stomach. I love the eggplant parmesan sandwich. Or the country ham plate."

I open my menu and Minnie's looks like a combination of a hamburger place mixed with Cracker Barrel. It smells amazing in here and the whole place is filled with the sounds of lots of people laughing and visiting over lunch.

We all quiet down while we study the menu and Ashten talks with one of the waitresses who comes by. "We'll need a few baskets of rolls over here," she tells her and the waitress nods.

"No problem, Ash. How's school going?"

She talks for a few more minutes about her students and their progress and then the waitress leaves.

"My cousin," Ashten says, nodding to the girl. "She's in college right now. Thinking of going into education too, though I keep telling her to come spend a few days in the class with me before she decides to do that. I've known too many teachers who quit six months into the school year."

"I couldn't do it," Luke says, shaking his head. "I got asked to come talk to an assembly one time about music stuff and I left there feeling nothing but awe for you guys. It's a hard profession."

Mike is nodding. "I couldn't do it, either."

"I can't stand children, so I definitely couldn't do it," Eliza declares.

"You work on the Mother Baby floor," I tell Eliza.

"Right."

"So, don't you technically work with children?" I ask her, grinning.

Eliza shakes her head. "There is a night and day difference between a newborn and a child," she says. "A newborn can't tell me they don't want to do something. They might try to tell me that, but I just tell the mothers their crying just means that they're cold or something and I just swaddle them up anyway."

I laugh. "Nurse of the year, right there."

"You know it."

Ashten's cousin comes back with two baskets piled high with buttery, incredibly soft and still steaming rolls.

I am immediately drooling.

"Rolls and honey butter," she says, setting them down. "You guys ready to order?"

Ashten looks around the table and I think everyone else has decided, so I quickly decide on the cheeseburger with a salad instead of the fries. If I'm going to be eating rolls too, I'll need the salad to counterbalance everything. My thirty-one year-old metabolism isn't my twenty-one year-old metabolism.

Everyone orders and digs into the rolls and, for a little bit, the only sound at the table is of people chewing.

"Holy cow," Eliza sighs after inhaling a roll.

"Wow." I am reaching for another roll before I can even fully form the word. "Oh my gosh, Ashten."

"What do I need to do to get the recipe for these rolls?" Eliza asks.

"You have to marry into the family," Ashten grins.

"Perfect. Introduce me to someone."

"The only single guy of a marriageable age right now is my cousin, Trevor," Ashten says.

"Trevor sounds like a wonderful man. Tell him I accept."

Ashten smirks. "He's nineteen and thinks he's going to be the next big rock and roll star."

"Hey, you never know," Luke pipes up. "I wanted to be a singer when I was nineteen, too. Now it pays all the bills."

"You've never heard my cousin sing," Ashten tells him. "I have heard you sing and let me just say that you don't have to worry about any competition coming from my family."

Luke grins. "So, what do you think, Eliza? Still interested?"

"I don't know. Let me think on it." She reaches for another roll and Mike stops her.

"I thought you had resolved this year not to make any rash decisions while consuming carbs," he says.

"I'm thinking through it. That means it isn't rash."

"Deciding to marry someone for a roll recipe is pretty rash," Mike says.

"Mike, I am a nurse. I specialize in rashes."

"I thought you specialized in infant care," Ashten grins.

I laugh. "Well, even if I got the recipe I wouldn't know what to do with it, so I'm going to help myself to another roll and just plan on working out tomorrow," I say. I slather the honey butter over the warm roll and it starts to melt upon impact.

Oh dear goodness.

I'm pretty sure these rolls will be served in heaven. I hope that Ashten's grandmother is planning on working up there.

"How many of these does she make a day?" I ask.

"You don't even want to know," Ashten says. "Grandma used to get up at four o'clock in the morning to start making them for the day. Now she pays one of my other cousins to do it all day long."

"How many cousins do you have?" Luke asks.

"Twelve. Eight of them work here." She shrugs. "I guess I technically do during the summers. And occasionally on the weekends. Especially during holiday weekends or around Christmas. Grandma is always looking for extra hands around then."

Eliza is busy chewing another roll. "So, if I get hired on for the Christmas season, could I get the recipe? I mean, I only work three shifts right now, occasionally four. That leaves me a lot of time to make rolls."

Ashten laughs. "You're ridiculous."

By the time we get back home, it's close to three o'clock. We spent way too long at Minnie's Diner, but with rolls like that, I know I'll be back there a lot. They just kept bringing the baskets of rolls, too. As soon as someone's hand would touch the last roll, another basket would appear.

I pull up to my house. Eliza rode back with Mike, but Ashten was coming by to drop off a couple of boxes she'd packed up so she didn't have to move them next weekend.

"Thanks for letting me do this. The less I have to cart over next weekend, the better," Ashten says, setting a couple of boxes in the garage. "My cousin is bringing his truck over to help me move the furniture. I'm pretty much just keeping my bedroom furniture, though. And my juicer."

I grin. "Nice priorities."

"Thanks. The couch was a hand-me-down anyway, so I'm giving it to the nineteen year-old cousin I was telling you about."

"Maybe he'll incorporate it into one of his album covers someday."

She laughs. "Right."

I hand her the keys and garage door opener. "Just consider it your house. You can come by anytime you need to."

"Thanks, Katie."

At five o'clock, I get a text from Eliza.

Soup?

I think I'm still kind of full from lunch, but I know if I don't eat now, I'll be starving when it's time for bed. I text her back and walk across the street a few minutes later.

Eliza opens the door and then goes into the kitchen, ladling two bowls of what looks like some kind of chicken chowder.

"Smells great," I say.

"Thanks. Thanks for coming to eat with me. Sometimes after Mike leaves, I get really lonely really quick."

I nod. "I could see that."

"It was just the two of us for so long, you know? Don't get me wrong, I love my independence, but it's sort of like a homesick thing. So, I'm coping the only way I know how." She slides on an oven mitt and pulls a cookie sheet of chocolate chip cookies out of the oven.

I shake my head at her. "I honestly don't see how you stay so skinny."

"You forget that I spend four days a week on a twelve hour shift where I barely have time to go to the bathroom, much less eat." She shrugs. "Half of the time, I'll get a package of peanut butter crackers and that will be it. Unless it's a slow day. Which rarely happens. So, I make sure I eat well on my days off."

"When do you work next?"

"I'm working tomorrow, Tuesday, Wednesday and Friday."

"Wow."

"Yep. Busy week. Speaking of which, I'll be late to Bible study on Wednesday. I don't get off until seven and that usually means I don't get home until eight."

I nod. "That's fine." It's my week to lead. At some point, I should probably do some prep work.

We carry our soup bowls to the living room and Eliza turns the TV onto to HGTV. "I could watch home remodeling shows all day long," she says, blowing on her soup. She pauses. "Actually, I *have* watched home remodeling shows all day long."

"It makes me want to rip out my bathrooms," I tell her, stirring my soup.

"And what? Use an outhouse?"

"No, redo them. I would take out the tile and put in granite counters and at least re-stain the cabinet or possibly replace it completely."

"Oh, got it. Yeah, it's hard to watch these shows, then go in and see laminate countertops," Eliza grins.

We watch as a couple with Texan accents rip out walls of a tiny, cottage-style house.

"So Luke seems nice," Eliza says.

I smile into my soup. I was wondering how long it would take her to bring up Luke. She actually lasted a lot longer than I thought she would.

"He does seem nice," I nod.

"How do you know him?"

I think about that question and then decide to tell her the whole story. "So, I met him first at Panera, but then his grandmother and my grandmother set us up on kind of a blind date, except they were both there for it."

"Okay then."

"Yeah."

"So, he's a wedding singer?"

I nod. "He's really good, too."

"And, another perk, he's a lot better looking than Adam Sandler."

"Also a good point," I grin.

Eliza eats a few bites of her soup. "So, what's the plan?"

I know what she's asking, but I don't know the answer, so I try evasiveness. "I'll probably finish my soup and then get a chocolate chip cookie."

"Not what I meant."

"I know." I knew it wouldn't work.

"Are you going to start dating Luke?"

"I don't know."

"What about the guy in New York?"

"I don't know."

"What about Mike? And our plan to be sisters?"

"Your plan," I correct. "And I don't know."

"You are just full of all kinds of knowledge today."

I set my empty soup bowl on her coffee table and pull my knees up to my chest with a long sigh. "Eliza...I don't know."

She grins. "Yeah. I got that."

"So, this kind of thing just doesn't, um, it doesn't happen to me."

"What kind of thing?"

"Men."

"Men don't happen to you?"

"Men being interested don't."

Eliza rolls her eyes. "Please. Katie, you're gorgeous, you are super kind and you can put your pants on the right way."

I grin. "These are the qualifications of having men be interested in you?"

"Yep. And actually, I'm not even sure you need those three. Sometimes it seems like just being female is enough. But my point is that even if it hasn't happened a lot in the past, it was only a matter of time before someone showed some interest."

I pick at my nails. "Hey, Eliza?"

"Yeah?"

"Can I ask you a question?"

She nods. "Sure."

"What if I find something wrong with all of these guys right now?"

She squints at me. "What do you mean?"

"I mean, what if this is it? Like, what if these are my choices and if I don't like any of them, I'm just doomed to a life of loneliness?"

Eliza sighs. "This isn't going back to that man who died in the flood, is it?"

"I mean, kind of."

"Katie, you have to let go of that analogy."

"Probably."

She looks at me, eyes thoughtful. "You know what I think you need to do? Just get away. Go out of town for a day, go drive around and look at the fall colors or something. Just be by yourself."

"I'm always by myself."

"No," Eliza says, still with that thoughtful expression. "I really don't think you are. I think you are often alone, but you aren't often by yourself."

"Aren't those the same thing?"

She pats my knee. "I'm going to tell you something my grandmother told me when I was fifteen years old. 'Eliza, you won't ever be content with someone if you can't learn how to be content by yourself first.'"

I just look at her. "I don't get it."

"You just finished the book you were editing, right?"

I nod.

"Okay. *Go.* Drive. Look at the fall colors. Take your Bible, a journal, a pen and some coffee. Don't do any work and leave your cell in the glove compartment." She nods to herself. "Yes, that's what you need. Just go. Okay?"

I don't think she would have accepted any other answer, so I just nod again. "Okay."

CHAPTER *Eighteen*

When I lived in New York and wanted to get outside and go exploring, there just wasn't a good place to go. Sometimes I would poke around Central Park, sometimes I would find a nice overlook by the ocean. But no matter where I went, I was surrounded by people and especially tourists. I was never alone. Which was ironic, considering how lonely I was.

Now, though, I push the button on the cruise control and lean back in my seat. The colors of the trees around me are breathtaking and I haven't seen another car for a few miles.

It's beautiful.

It's about nine-thirty on Monday morning. I did what Eliza suggested and threw my cell in the glove compartment. I'd send Joe an email this morning and told him I was taking the morning off, so if he needed to get a hold of me, write what he was going to ask me on a post-it note and I would be back this afternoon.

If I had to guess, I bet he is panicking. Joe doesn't live more than a couple of seconds unplugged from technology and it terrifies him when someone he talks to often doesn't immediately reply back.

I have no idea where I'm going, but I drive for a good thirty minutes before I find a little clearing on the side of the road at the top of a hill. The view is incredible and I pull over, climb out and lean back against the hood of my car, adjusting my sunglasses on my face.

I wish I'd brought my good camera. I break the rule and pull my phone out for a minute to take a couple pictures and then I stick it back in the glove compartment. I push myself up on top of the hood of my car, tucking my knees into my chest and looking at the reds, golds and oranges around me, shining in the early morning sun.

You honestly cannot beat Missouri in the fall.

"Well, Lord."

I don't say anything else for a long minute. Yesterday morning's sermon is still heavy on my heart.

My whole life, all I've wanted is to get married. I totally thought I would be one of those people who got married right after college and had a couple of kids by this point in my life.

And instead, I've watched friend after friend walk down the aisle into marital bliss and leave me behind in my sea of wedding invitations and wrapping paper. I've started buying shower gifts when they are on sale rather than when someone registers for them. You only have to buy so many hand mixers before you realize that everyone basically registers for the same brand of things.

I would leave their weddings and cry all the way home, all the way up to my apartment and all the way to my closet where I would hang my bridesmaid's dress.

"How long, Lord?" I would beg and then immediately I would feel guilty. Especially when I would meet with those married friends for coffee and they would tell me all the hard parts about marriage. They would tell me how lucky I was that I could still afford to go to Starbucks whenever I wanted to and I could watch whatever I wanted to watch on the TV at all times.

Then came the baby wave and I bought eight different baby monitors in two months. And I would visit the little cherubs in the hospital and bring the parents meals and again cry all the way home. I was still asking "how long, Lord?" And I was still overcome with guilt, because now I met with those tired parents and heard all about how lucky I was to sleep through the night and not have stretch marks covering my lower midsection.

Over and over again, time after time, week after week, I would hear it constantly.

The mantra.

"God is saving someone *really* special for you, Katie."

"Just keep trusting Him, Katie. I know He has someone out there for you."

And then when the weeks, months and years went by:

"Maybe there is some unresolved sin in your life, Katie? Maybe that's why God isn't blessing you with a husband?"

"You need to start putting God first so that He can give you the gift of marriage."

"Just wait. As soon as you stop looking for it, it will happen."

I'd hear story after story about how so-and-so did one of the above things and boom, like magic, they were married the next week.

So, I would throw myself into Bible studies and accountability groups. I'd spend my whole weekends serving at the homeless shelters and food kitchens. I went through my closet on a monthly basis and donated all the extras I could find to a women's crisis shelter.

And still, no one came along.

I think that's when things started going south for me.

Didn't God see I loved Him and wanted to serve Him alongside a husband? Didn't He see that the best plan for my life was to meet someone, fall in love and raise babies who would also love Him? I've sat through sermon after sermon about how our greatest mission field is at home. Hard to believe when I'm the only one at the breakfast table.

And now, here are three men right in front of me.

I think about all of them and sigh into the cold, fall air.

J.T., with his classic New York style and his fairly easy-to-talk-to personality. Maybe there wasn't a lot of spark, but it is a spark, after all, that starts fires big enough to burn down cities. Maybe a slightly boring existence is better.

I rub my temples. Dear goodness, I am going to become Charlotte.

Then, there's Mike. Hard working, overprotective, worrywart Mike. He seems super nice, but also super concerned about pretty much everything. But you know, maybe that could be a good thing. I'd rather have someone who was worried about me than someone who wasn't. Right?

Of course, it could also be stifling and annoying. Especially considering I've lived over a decade fending for myself.

And then, there's Luke.

I look out at the trees.

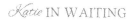

"What about Luke, Lord?"

Luke is kind. Luke is funny. And there's actually maybe a little chemistry between us.

So, why doesn't it feel right?

I mean, shouldn't I be home, humming "So This Is Love" as I tidy up my house and I don't know, make a dress out of my drapes or something? Shouldn't I be giddy with excitement over potential love after all these years of nothing?

Instead, I just feel confused.

And alone.

I squint out at the trees and then open my Bible next to me. Maybe God has some special verse picked out for me, something that He's been saving in His back pocket for just a time like this. Maybe it's something like, *Katie, when you read this, here's exactly what you need to do in a convenient, five-step plan that also includes a necessary step for eating chocolate.*

Maybe it will hold reassurances of His plan for my life and His hand over what's going on right now. Maybe the name "Luke" will even be in there and it will be like this heavenly sign that I'm supposed to end up with him.

I open my Bible to Jeremiah and read the first verses I find.

For thus says the Lord, "Your wound is incurable and your injury is serious. There is no one to plead your cause; no healing for your sore, no recovery for you."

"Really?" I say out loud to the trees. "Seriously, that's it?"

Not even a bird answers me back.

Wednesday night I am somehow surrounded by twelve people in my own living room.

If we continue to double every week, we are going to need to move this little soiree to a park before too long. And as much of a fan as I am of meeting in a park, I don't think that November is the time to be meeting there.

Frostbite and all that.

I set chocolate chip cookies on a plate right as the coffeepot beeps to let me know it's done.

Ashten comes into the kitchen, looking over her shoulder into the living room as she walks over to me. "So, who are these people?" she asks me in a low voice.

"Honestly, I have no idea."

"Where did they come from?"

I shrug. "Aren't those two the girls from last week?"

"Yeah. Maybe they invited everyone."

"You didn't?"

She shakes her head. "I only invited one person and she isn't here."

"Who did you invite?"

"One of the teachers at my school." Ashten looks around. "Maybe she'll still come. She's kind of floundering right now. I think a study would be good for her. I'll introduce you if she makes it."

I am starting to get nervous about teaching, especially since my heart hasn't really been in the right place after my drive the other day. Instead of making me see things more clearly, it just made everything more fuzzy.

"Hey, you okay?" Ashten asks, nudging me with her elbow. "You seem kind of down today."

I shrug. "I'm all right."

"Sure?"

I nod, rather than half-lie again. Which I guess could also be a lie. I change the subject. "Did you bring over more boxes?"

"Yep. Got them all loaded into the guest room. I have a bunch of kitchen stuff from my apartment I thought I would just bring over and if we have duplicates, I'll either save it or donate it. Most of it was secondhand to begin with."

I nod. "Sounds good."

Ashten looks at the crowd. "Well. Shall we?"

"Yep. Let me get my notes."

I grab my Bible and my notes on First John. I'm following in Eliza's footsteps and leading more by guiding the conversation rather than actually teaching. Which is probably better, considering my current state of heart right now, anyway.

"Hey everyone, thank you for coming," I say, pulling one of my dining chairs into the family room since all the seats, including a few on the floor, have been taken. "We are definitely growing. I'm Katie, in case I haven't met you. So, we've been talking through First John, so if you could turn there with me, we can get started." I say a quick prayer.

I pick up at the point where Eliza left off. "'These things we write, so that our joy may be made complete. This is the message that we have heard from Him and announce to you, that God is Light and in Him there is no darkness at all.'"

I stop reading and look around at the twenty-four eyes looking back at me.

Talk about intimidating.

I clear my throat. "So, um, what do you guys think these verses mean?"

One of the new girls pipes up. I don't remember her name. "I think it is comforting, you know? I mean, if God is Light and there isn't any darkness in Him, then we know that He really is taking care of us. He really does have a plan for us and it's a good plan. And I think that's what it means when it talks about joy. We can have complete joy because He is only Light. He is only good."

She quiets down and I can feel my throat closing up.

I struggle to swallow the lump and move on. I just stare at my Bible for a good thirty seconds of silence, the words swimming as I blink back tears.

Ashten obviously notices what's going on and starts talking. "Great point there. I really like what you said. I think the joy being complete may also refer to the earlier verses which I'll read real quick for those of you who missed last week."

She takes over and I sit quietly for most of the rest of the study. Ashten prays, people eat cookies and mingle and then they all finally leave, except for Ashten. She closes the door behind the last girl and looks at me as I wash the coffeepot.

"Fine, hmm?" she says.

"Fine."

She leans against the cabinets, resting her elbows on the counter, clasping her hands together. "Want to talk about it?"

I look at her and her compassionate blue eyes. How is it that I just met these girls? They've quickly become like sisters to me.

"Do you ever...?" I start and then I stop, setting the rinsed coffeepot on a clean towel to dry.

"Do I ever?"

"Do you ever just get anxious about what God is really thinking?"

She chuckles. "Um, do I ever not?"

"Really?"

"Sure. I think we all get anxious to know God's plans for our lives."

"Eliza seems pretty chill about everything."

Ashten grins. "Eliza is a different breed of animal."

I smile.

"Is this about that guy we sat with at church?"

I shrug. "I guess it is in a way."

"What's going on with him?"

I sigh and lean back against the dishwasher. "We went out on one date. And I guess we had another dinner together with our grandparents."

Ashten grins. "Well, that's very *Little House on the Prairie* of you."

"Thanks."

"So, what's the problem?"

"On paper? There isn't one. He's sweet. He's a Christian."

"Not bad to look at, either," Ashten grins.

"And that."

"There seemed like there was some chemistry between you guys at church," Ashten says and I shrug.

"I think so."

"So, the problem is that he's too perfect on paper?"

I sigh. "I don't know what the problem is. It just doesn't..." I shake my head. "I guess it just doesn't feel like I thought it would."

"What are you talking about?"

"I just kind of always thought that someday when I met the right person, I would feel...I don't know. Something."

"I thought you said there was chemistry?" Ashten says.

"I mean, kind of." I think about how it is to be around Luke. I really like being around him. He makes me laugh. And there's definitely more there than I ever had talking with J.T.

Poor guy.

Ashten is studying me intently and it's starting to make me nervous. I tuck my hair behind my ears. "What?" I ask her.

"Can I say something?"

I'm not sure my permission is going to change what she does, but I nod. "Sure."

"I think you've spent your whole life waiting for something that doesn't really exist."

I just look at her. "What are you talking about?"

"I mean, you've mentioned that you've wanted to get married since you were really small, right?"

I nod. "You're saying marriage doesn't exist?"

"I'm saying that love the way you think it exists doesn't exist."

"Are you encouraging me to be Charlotte?"

"What?"

I rub my cheek. "Eliza told me that settling for a guy who doesn't have sparks going off around him is like me turning into Charlotte and marrying Mr. Collins just for security."

Ashten grins. "That sounds like something she would say. No, I'm not encouraging you to marry Mr. Collins, Katie. I'm just saying that I think you've been waiting for this thing for so long, you don't even recognize it anymore. I honestly feel like Mr. Right could come up and kick you in the face and you still wouldn't recognize him. I think you have this imaginary idea of what he should look like or be like or what it would feel like to be around him, when it may not be like that."

I just look at her.

She shrugs and pats the counter. "Anyway, it's just my theory. I'm guilty of it, too. I think it's our generation. We grew up on too many Disney princesses and their storybook, idealistic romances. And now, when the man we are dating even so much as sneezes weird, we're running for the hills."

I smile.

"And, to answer your original question, yes, I get anxious. I really worry sometimes God has this plan for me to marry some guy who's ugly and annoying and we are going to spend our lives bickering." She smiles. "But like my dad likes to remind me, if he wouldn't pick someone like that for me, why do I think that God, who loves me more than my dad, would do that?"

I don't have an answer for her.

She straightens. "All right. Well, I need to head out. I've got a meeting before school tomorrow." She steps over and pulls me into a hug. "Love you, Katie."

"Love you, Ashten."

"I'll see you soon."

I lock the door behind her and get ready for bed, her words still running through my mind.

CHAPTER *Nineteen*

Friday morning, my phone buzzes in a call from a number I don't recognize.

"Hello?"

"You are one hard woman to get a hold of." Luke's voice fills my ear. "I have been searching for your number like when I would pretend to be a detective as a nine year-old. It didn't help that my grandfather can't hear the phone ring, my grandmother never returns phone calls and your grandmother is apparently the busiest person on the planet."

I smile. "Hi Luke."

"Hey. So, I noticed that you weren't at Panera on Monday."

After my drive that day, I hadn't really been in the mood for Panera, but I don't tell Luke that. "No, I couldn't make it there this week."

"Well, I was thinking that I needed to eat lunch tomorrow and you needed to eat lunch tomorrow and so maybe, we could potentially eat those lunches together."

I smile. "Oh, yeah?"

"Yeah. So, are you available then?"

I think about what Ashten said about not recognizing what is right in front of me and I nod. "I can probably do that. Ashten is moving in this weekend so some of my availability might depend on what she needs from me."

"That will be good for you guys. I'm really glad she's moving in with you. Okay. So, let's go get breakfast instead and I'll come over and help move her in."

"You don't need to do that," I protest. There's this thought in the back of my head that if he treats his car so badly, maybe he wouldn't be able to neatly and cleanly move someone into my house.

I've seen the way Ashten has been setting boxes in my garage and the guest room. The boxes in the garage are alphabetized.

I knew I liked her.

"I would love to help," Luke says. "I love to help people move. I hate moving myself, but helping other people move is one of my specialties. I've got a wedding Saturday night, so I'll need to leave about three o'clock, but I would really like to help."

"Um. Okay." I'm not sure who Ashten has helping her. I know she had mentioned one of her cousins.

"Great! Can I pick you up about nine then?"

I think Ashten said she would probably be over with the first load around ten-thirty, so that would work. And I hear Luke's unspoken request to get my address.

I think through it and nod. "Sure." I tell him my address.

"Great!" he says, sounding awfully chipper for it being a workday morning. "I will see you at nine tomorrow then. Have a great day, Katie!"

We hang up and I spend the rest of the day finishing my initial read-through of the new book. I always take my time with this part, making a ridiculous amount of notes. By the time I'm done, I usually know the eye color of the most minuscule characters. But it's helpful, because occasionally an author will forget some of those details and a character's eyes will change from brown to blue over the course of the novel.

I'm not claiming to be a medical professional, but I'm fairly certain people's eyes stop changing color when they are still in the toddler stage.

At five-thirty, I pull on my UGG boots and drive the couple of minutes to Gram's house for dinner.

She opens the door and just looks at me.

"I know, I know, I'm sorry," I say, holding up my hands. "I'll try to remember to use my key next time."

"I will believe that when I see it," Gram says. "And what are you wearing?"

"Clothes?"

"Those are not clothes."

I look down at my leggings and tunic-style sweater. "What are they?"

"I don't know, but if you were wearing that outfit one hundred and fifty years ago, you might have been stoned."

"Gram, everything's covered."

"I just don't understand this phase of everything needing to be skin tight."

"My sweater isn't skin tight." I shrug. "And besides, I thought skinny jeans and leggings were throwbacks to the 80s."

"I didn't like them then, either," Gram says, walking into the kitchen.

"Surely you like this look better than the grunge look."

"What's a grunge?"

"Not 'a' grunge. Just grunge. It's what we went through in the 90s. The huge baggy pants that all the guys had to hold at the crotch so they wouldn't fall down around their ankles as they walked?"

Gram just sighs. "Sometimes I thank the good Lord that in Paradise, we will be given our heavenly suits and we won't have all these ridiculous people in Hollywood telling us what looks good and what doesn't."

I sit at Gram's island counter and grin. "Heavenly suits?"

"Honey, surely you know that we will all be dressed like we are in a Fred Astaire movie in heaven."

"I'm not sure I'll enjoy wearing a Fred Astaire suit for all of eternity."

"You can dress like Ginger Rogers. Or Audrey Hepburn." Gram patted her hips. "I fully intend on having Ginger's hips in heaven."

"I think Audrey wore skinny pants, Gram."

"No, Audrey Hepburn wore cigarette pants. Totally different."

"Mm-hmm."

"Don't sass your grandmother."

I grin. "Yes ma'am. It smells good in here, Gram."

"I made green chile cheese chicken enchilada casserole. I got the recipe from your New Mexico relatives."

I frown. "What New Mexico relatives?"

"My third cousin Margaret and her family."

"Are third cousins really even considered relatives? And wouldn't your third cousin be basically the same relation to me as someone I meet at Walmart?"

"There you go sassing again."

"Sorry."

Gram pulls on an oven mitt and slides a huge Pyrex dish with a layer of bubbling cheddar cheese on top of it out of the oven. I peer over at it as best as I can from the stool. "Wow."

"Margaret is quite the chef."

"Must run in the family," I say, nodding to Gram.

"I don't even really consider third cousins family, so I don't know what you are talking about," Gram says, grinning at me.

"Anyone ever mentioned how difficult you are to talk to?"

Gram smiles, pulling over a package of flour tortillas. "Your Pop-Pop used to tell me that all the time."

"Surely more people are coming tonight and you aren't expecting us to eat all this food, right?"

"Leftovers for you this week," Gram says, shaking her head. "I used the mild sauce because I've heard that too much of the spicier chile can give you indigestion and if you're going to be eating this for a week, I don't want you to spend the week in the bathroom."

"Thanks for watching out for my digestion."

"What are grandmothers for?" She joins me at the counter and slides a paper plate over towards me.

I smile at Gram. As much fun as it is to have company at her house, I really enjoy the nights where it is just the two of us relaxing together after the week.

"How was your day?" Gram asks.

"It was fine."

"Have you seen that Luke fellow yet?"

"Sure, Gram, I've seen him a few times."

She rolls her eyes. "You know what I mean. Did he ask you out on a date? Or whatever you people do these days?"

I nod. "We went out."

"Good. How was it?"

"His car is pretty gross."

Gram shakes her head. "Remember what I told you about finding a malleable man," she tells me. "Does he seem messy in every area? Because goodness knows it didn't look like he'd ever used a comb when he was over here."

"He uses a comb." We pray and I take a few bites of my enchiladas, which are amazing, like I knew they would be. I look over at Gram. "Hey, Gram?"

"Yes, honey?"

"How did you know Pop-Pop was the right one?"

"What are you talking about?"

I try to think about a different way to phrase it. "How did you know that Pop-Pop was the one that you should marry?"

Gram shakes her head. "Oh honey, that was so long ago."

"You don't remember?"

"I didn't say that. But, things are different now. You young people think too much."

I smile at her. "So, are you implying that I shouldn't think about who I marry? I should just up and get hitched to the first person to walk through the door?"

"Oh, I wouldn't go that far. Sometimes Walter from maintenance pops by to fix a light bulb for me. Goodness knows, I wouldn't wish him on you. Though he's already married, so you should be safe."

"Well, that's good to know."

"So, did Luke propose or something?" Gram asks me.

I shake my head. "Oh no, no, no. No. Just thinking. And needing a little bit of advice. Things have been…I don't know." I shake my head again. "Weird. Things have been weird lately. And I'm getting conflicting things from my friends."

"Well, what are friends for except to cause conflict?" Gram says. "I mean, look at my friends. Frieda is basically a walking conflict right there."

I grin. "True."

"So, what is the advice you've been getting?"

"One of my friends…Eliza? I don't think you've met her."

"I don't think so, but I do love the name. One of my dear friends in grade school was named Eliza."

"Anyway, Eliza says that if I continue dating someone whom I don't have a ton of chemistry with, I'm basically signing myself up for a lifetime of being married to Mr. Collins from *Pride and Prejudice*."

"Well now, he was a nasty man," Gram says, shaking her head.

"Agreed."

"So, what do your other friends say?"

"Just one. Ashten? She's the one who is moving in this weekend." I'd told Gram about her on the phone.

Gram nods. "Okay."

"So Ashten thinks I'm overthinking everything and that I've created this idea of what I think Mr. Right should be like and he doesn't really exist."

"Mr. Wright? Who is that?"

"No, Right like the Right One. Not Wright like a last name."

Gram nods. "Got it. Well, honey, what do you think Mr. Right should be like?"

I shrug, poking at my enchiladas with my fork. "I don't know. Tall, dark and handsome?"

"I think that's how you describe coffee, honey. Not men."

I smile. "So, it's basically the opposite advice as Eliza's, right? I mean, Ashten is all about not overlooking the people that God has right in front of you and Eliza is all about waiting for the one who causes fireworks to go off."

"Now that just sounds dangerous with the drought going on across the country."

I nod. "Agreed."

Gram grins and pats my hand. "So, this is why you wanted to know about your grandfather."

"Yeah." I shrug. "I mean, I don't even know if I've ever heard the story of how you two met."

"Oh, surely you have heard that one, Katie."

"I don't know if I have."

Gram smiles and there's nostalgia in her expression. "I met him at a bus stop."

I definitely haven't ever heard this story. "Seriously?"

"Seriously. I can still remember the day like it just happened. He was wearing the one suit he owned on his way home from trying to find work. Work was hard to come by back then, what with the war just ending a bit before that. Anyway, that day he'd just happened to find a job with AT&T and he was so excited that he asked me to go out to dinner to celebrate with him."

"And you'd never met him before?" I ask.

"Nope."

"Did you go?"

"Sure," Gram says, shrugging. "He had a job, after all. And a suit. And we all know my feelings on suits."

I smile and try to imagine my grandparents back in the day. I've seen pictures of both of them when they first got married. Gram was every bit as thin and beautiful as Ginger Rogers and Pop-Pop was tall and skinny too, barely recognizable when it came to the slightly pudgy grandfather I remembered. He was already balding as an early twenty-something.

"How long did you date before you got engaged?" I ask.

"Oh, about three months or so."

"*Three* months?"

Gram shrugs again. "Sure. Why not? We even took our time. I already knew everything I needed to know about him after a month. We had lunch every day together during our lunch breaks because our offices were right across a little lake from each other. We would pack something we could eat while we were walking, and we'd walk this little path around the lake and eat our sandwiches and visit."

"Yeah, but three months?" I shake my head. "That just seems really fast."

"I suppose it is fast for these days. But back then, things were just different. Simpler. We didn't have eighty-five different forms of communication with each other. We didn't spend half our time together staring at our cell phones or watching television. And we didn't start dating until we knew we were in the position to get married." She shakes her head. "So, I would probably vouch that I knew him better after one month than most people know each other after a few years these days."

I nod. "True, I guess." I let Gram eat some of her enchiladas. "So, how did you know he was the one?" I ask again.

"Well, I didn't hate him. He had a good job. He loved the Lord." Gram looks at me. "What else did I need to know?"

I grin. "That's it? No sparks?"

"Honey, your Pop-Pop had so many sparks coming out the back of the Buick he bought after he got his first paycheck that we didn't need any," Gram says.

I laugh.

CHAPTER *Twenty*

Saturday morning dawns sunshiny and cool and it's like the day was made for apple cider.

Perfect day to move in.

I always worry about moving when someone is using an open-bed truck because you never know when a freak rain storm will pop up and all of a sudden, you're having to buy a new mattress.

And those aren't cheap.

I hop in and out of the shower, comb out my hair and add in some curling mousse and volumizing spray. There's no sense in spending a lot of time on it this morning, even though Luke and I are going out to breakfast. It's just going to end up in a bun when I'm helping Ashten later.

Luke is right on time. "Hey Katie," he says, smiling on my doorstep. "Ready for breakfast?"

I am starving, but I just smile politely and nod. "Definitely." I usually eat breakfast pretty quick after I wake up, so now my stomach is all confused and worried, like I'm not going to feed it today.

"There's this little place near the river that has pretty good pancakes or we could try and get to Ashten's grandparents' diner. I think we could be back before she comes over. What do you think?" Luke asks, opening the passenger door for me.

"Are you sure we have time for Minnie's Diner?" I ask, trying to close my eyes to the mess on the floorboards. Maybe if I just pretend it isn't there, it won't bother me.

He shrugs. "We could try it. It doesn't take too long to drive there and the roads are not going to be crowded today since it's the weekend. Want to go there?"

"Sure."

"Sounds good." He closes my door, climbs in the driver's seat and starts down the road toward the highway. "So Ashten is going to be at your house around ten-thirty?"

I nod. "That's what she said yesterday."

"Perfect. We should have plenty of time."

He talks for a little bit about the wedding he's going to be doing that evening. "They were a last minute booking after a last minute cancellation," he says.

"That's a bummer."

"The booking?"

"The cancellation."

He nods and then shrugs. "Well, actually, after meeting the couple, I would say it is probably for the best. You know how those couples you can tell right from the beginning it isn't going to work out? That was them in a nutshell. So, it was kind of good news to get that phone call. It's a lot better to break off an engagement than to be in a marriage where you aren't compatible."

"That's true."

"And this other couple just found out that he has to be deployed earlier than they expected, so they had to move their wedding up five months."

"Okay, now that's really sad."

He nods. "I imagine there will be a lot of tears tonight."

"That doesn't sound like a very fun evening."

He shakes his head. "You know, it will be good. Like I said, I really enjoy being a part of one of the biggest days of their lives. Even if it is sad, this is a night that they will remember for the rest of their lives. So, it's important to make it the best I can."

Luke has a kind heart.

We get to the diner and I'm staring at the biggest plates of waffles covered in a mountain of strawberries, blueberries, peaches and raspberries a few minutes later. The waitress sets three different kinds of syrup pitchers in front of me and refreshes our coffees. "Let me know if you need anything else," she says. I wonder if she is related to Ashten.

Luke prays a short, simple prayer for the meal and then we start eating. I am stuffed before I've even finished half of the waffles.

"Can I get you more coffee?" the waitress asks as I lean back from the table.

"I'm good, thank you," I say, waving a hand. If I put one more thing in my mouth, it's not going to end well for anyone.

Luke scrapes his plate. For being as thin as he is, the boy can put away food. "So, what does this week look like for you?"

"It's pretty normal, so far. I'm working on a new book with a new author. Wednesday night, Eliza, Ashten and I started a little Bible study that meets at my house." I nod to Luke. "You're welcome to come. It's on First John. I think Ashten is facilitating the discussion this week."

Luke grins. "I'd like that. I'll be there."

"Sounds good."

We talk small talk and it's nice. I don't know if it's the talks with Eliza, Ashten and Gram or what, but I feel like I'm on hyperdrive as far as noticing whether or not there are any sparks when we are talking.

I honestly can't tell. He's nice. He's kind. He seems to love Jesus.

For Gram, that would have probably been enough to warrant a ring.

Luke looks at his watch. "Well, we should probably start heading back if we are going to beat Ashten to your house," he says, nodding to the waitress who brings us over the check. I offer to pay, but he waves me off. "Are you kidding? I asked you to breakfast. Okay, let's head out."

He drives me back to my house and we haven't even made it to the front door before a gray Silverado truck drives past my house and then backs up into the driveway, a full load precariously balanced in the back. Ashten's car is right behind it, pulling up behind Luke's 4Runner on the front curb.

"Hey," Ashten says, grinning, hopping out of her car excitedly.

"Good morning," I smile at her.

"Katie, this is my cousin, Trevor."

The nineteen year-old wannabe rock-and-roll star, if I remember right. I smile and reach for the kid's hand. "Nice to meet you."

He flicks his long hair out of his eyes. "Yeah. Same."

"This is Luke."

The guys kind of half wave to each other and then Trevor goes around and opens the tailgate. Ashten and I open the front door. We get the furniture in the living room pushed back away from the walkway, so the boys can get to the guest room without too much trouble.

It only takes about thirty minutes for all of her furniture from the truck to get loaded into her room.

"You guys are fast," Ashten says, looking around her room with wide eyes. Everything fits in here perfectly and I even had the guys scoot my desk over in the office so her desk can go in there too.

"It's not like you're home during the day when I'm working anyway," I told her over her protests about my work space.

"Well, I'm going to take off," Trevor says, flicking his hair out of his eyes again.

"Thank you so much, Trevor."

"Yeah, no problem, Ashten. Nice place."

"Thanks!" she grins.

Luke heads out as well and Ashten raises her eyebrows at me as we close the door after the boys.

"So, Luke again, hmm?" she says, grinning.

"He asked if I wanted to get breakfast this morning," I tell her.

"Apparently, you said yes."

"I thought a lot about what you said and I don't want to miss something that's right in front of me," I tell her.

She looks at me. "I said that?"

"You said I have created something of what I think love looks like and you don't think that's it."

Ashten nods. "Right, but I don't remember saying you should settle for someone just because he's there. A relationship needs other things besides the convenience of the person being around."

Ashten heads back to her room and starts unpacking her sheets and bedspread. I help her make the bed, then get the clothes that she'd laid across the backseat of her car, still on the hangers.

"It just seemed like the easiest way to transfer clothes from one place to another," Ashten grins.

"Very true," I nod.

"Hey, Katie, I've got this. I don't want you to spend your whole day trying to get me moved in."

I shrug. "I don't have any other plans."

"Why don't you go for a walk or something? Just take some time to think or pray or read your Bible. Just get away for a little bit?"

I look at Ashten and considering the way it ended the last time I tried to get away from things, I'm not sure I want to do that.

"Well," I stall.

"Please Katie? I know you could use it."

I know I could, too.

I finally nod. "Okay. You're sure?"

"Positive. I'll see you later. Have a good afternoon!"

I grab my Bible again and get in the car, pushing my sunglasses on my face and just looking out the windshield.

Where should I go?

I start driving and end up toward the downtown area by the river. A walk along the river sounds nice. The city recently redid a lot of the walkways down here, so everything is nice and clean. The trees are in their fall glory and I'm definitely not the only person out here. Dogs are happily panting away on leashes in front of their owners, bicyclists zoom past yelling "on the left!" as they pass the joggers and walkers, old couples are strolling along, hand in hand, taking in the fresh air and the crispiness of fall.

It's beautiful.

I tuck my Bible under my arm and keep about the same pace as the elderly couple in front of me, who also appears to not be in a hurry. Bikes whiz past me, joggers go around me, but I just look at the river and the trees and inhale the cold air.

Well, Lord. Maybe we can just start over.

Here's the thing. I don't want to insult the deity and greatness and majesty of God. And I don't want Him to think I'm disrespectful for questioning things, especially His plan.

But, I'm questioning things. Especially His plan.

I look at the couple in front of me and the way that their hands just sort of fit together after all these years.

See, Lord? I want that. I could potentially have that with Luke.

"On your left!" A bicycle flies past me.

Or with J.T. Or with Mike. For the first time in my life, there are possibilities. So, what do I do, Lord? See where they go? Continue to wait for something better to come along?

I remember back when I was in college, we had to write an essay about the thing that scared us the most. I think it was around Halloween time. People wrote about zombies, snakes, stuff like that.

I could have summed up my essay in one sentence.

I am scared of ending up alone.

Alone.

Even the word is scary to me. It's scarier now than it ever has been before.

Jesus, what if I end up alone? What if I never find the "right" one and it's just me for the rest of my life? What if I never have babies? What if I grow to be this old woman without family to take care of me as I age?

I think about Gram and how independent she is, but I know the day is coming when she won't be able to do all that she does. It was a big reason why I moved here, so I could help out more when that day arrived.

I find an empty little bench overlooking the river. I sit and just look over the water.

I'm holding my Bible in my hands, but I'm scared I'm going to find another random verse that is just going to confuse me more.

I flip to the back and find a note in a purple pen on the back inside cover. I don't even remember writing it, but there's two references in Isaiah written down.

Might as well read them.

The first reference is in Isaiah 41. I start reading it and tears immediately fill my eyes.

"'Do not fear, for I am with you; do not anxiously look about you, for I am your God. I will strengthen you, surely I will help you, surely I will uphold you with My righteous right hand.'"

Do not fear.

The words sink into my heart and I flip over a few chapters to find the other verse in chapter 62.

"You will also be a crown of beauty in the hand of the LORD, and a royal diadem in the hand of your God. It will no longer be said to you, 'Forsaken,' nor to your land will it any longer be said, 'Desolate'; but you will be called, 'My delight is in her,' and your land, 'Married'; for the LORD delights in you, and to Him your land will be married... And as the bridegroom rejoices over the bride, so your God will rejoice over you."

I sit there on the bench by the river and tears slowly drip onto the pages of my Bible.

I have been terrified. Completely petrified of ending up alone.

And here, by this river, it's like Jesus is sitting next to me and telling me that I am not alone.

I have never been alone.

All those years of waiting, and Jesus was already here. All those years of wishing for something different and God already knew I would be here today. All those times of sitting in a wedding and wishing that I had a man looking at me the way the groom was staring love-struck at the bride, and God was already rejoicing over me.

Jesus, this is what I needed to hear.

But at the same time…

I look up over the river.

I still want to meet someone, Lord.

I know He knows.

I walk a little farther, thinking, praying, re-reading the words I read on the bench. And I drive home, turning the music down on the speakers, listening to the quiet and thinking more.

I walk inside my house and it smells amazing. I follow my nose and the sound of voices into the kitchen. Ashten and Eliza are busy cooking, setting out three napkins and spoons on my kitchen table.

"There she is," Ashten smiles at me. "We were just about to call you. I made soup and Eliza brought over some muffins. Are you hungry?"

"The correct answer is yes," Eliza says, grinning at me. "I pushed something weird on the website where I found the muffin recipe and accidentally tripled it. You'd better each eat a dozen muffins tonight."

"Tough luck, Eliza. I am not eating twelve muffins tonight."

"See, you are like the perfect teacher, Ashten, restating what I said in your own words," Eliza grins.

I watch them both, listening to their chatter and smiling.

Jesus, I'm not alone.

No matter what the future holds, I know I won't be. I have friends. I have Gram. I have Jesus.

And that, for now, for always, is enough.

THE *End*

Don't miss the continuing story in Once Upon Eliza, *coming Summer 2016!*

Made in the USA
Lexington, KY
04 August 2016